DRYLANDS

Thea Astley is one of Australia's most celebrated writers. Three times she has won the Miles Franklin Award – in 1962 for *The Well Dressed Explorer*, in 1965 for *The Slow Natives*, and in 1972 for *The Acolyte*. In 1989 she was awarded the Patrick White Award. Other awards include the 1986 ALS Gold Medal for *Beachmasters*, the 1988 Steele Rudd Award for *It's Raining in Mango*, the 1990 NSW Premier's Prize for *Reaching Tin River*, and the 1996 *Age* Book of the Year Award and the FAW Australian Unity Award for *The Multiple Effects of Rainshadow*.

Thea Astley held a position as Fellow in Australian Literature at Macquarie University until 1980, when she retired to write full time. She now lives in the hills on the south coast of New South Wales.

THEA ASTLEY
DRYLANDS

a book for the world's last reader

PENGUIN BOOKS

Penguin Books Australia Ltd
487 Maroondah Highway, PO Box 257
Ringwood, Victoria 3134, Australia
Penguin Books Ltd
Harmondsworth, Middlesex, England
Penguin Putnam Inc.
375 Hudson Street, New York, New York 10014, USA
Penguin Books Canada Limited
10 Alcorn Avenue, Toronto, Ontario, Canada M4V 3B2
Penguin Books (NZ) Ltd
Cnr Rosedale and Airborne Roads, Albany, Auckland, New Zealand
Penguin Books (South Africa) (Pty) Ltd
5 Watkins Street, Denver Ext 4, 2094, South Africa
Penguin Books India (P) Ltd
11, Community Centre, Panchsheel Park, New Delhi 110 017, India

First published by Penguin Books Australia Ltd 1999
This edition published by Penguin Books Australia Ltd 2000

1 3 5 7 9 10 8 6 4 2

Design by Ellie Exarchos, Penguin Design Studio
Cover photograph by Eric Algra
Typeset in 11.5/17 pt Granjon by Post Pre-press Group, Brisbane, Queensland
Made and printed in Australia by Australian Print Group, Maryborough, Victoria

National Library of Australia
Cataloguing-in-Publication data:

Astley, Thea, 1925– .
Drylands.

ISBN 0 14 028380 3.

I. Title.

A823.3

www.penguin.com.au

Acknowledgements

The author wishes to thank the Literature Fund of the Australia Council for the Creative Arts Fellowship which helped in the writing of this book.

The quotes from D. H. Lawrence on page 15 are taken from *A Selection from Phoenix*, edited by A. A. Inglis, published by Penguin, 1971, reproduced by permission of Laurence Pollinger Limited and the Estate of Frieda Lawrence Ravagli.

MEANWHILE . . .

'I've never sailed the Amazon. I've never reached Brazil,' she quoted, and I've never been to a literary festival or a poetry reading, she thought, and listened to poets read, awed by their own genius.

A lot of things she hadn't done. Sitting now, useless maybe, in her upstairs flat with a view of the town's pub, grocery store, unused picture show, council building and primary school skulking by the wattles near where the creek used to flow. But I might write a book – something – she decided, having the wherewithal: table, typewriter, a new ream of paper, and angry ideas.

And alone-time in the hot evenings.

Past fifty, she admitted. And had really done nothing except move from one day to the next, accepting the vagaries of personal weather. These were written on her anxious face, blinked behind her glasses; they turned up the corners of her mouth that tried to conceal its amusement in a town that went for the most explicit of laughs.

All she had to do was insert a page in the typer, adjust her kitchen chair, flex her fingers as if she were about to crash into the Rach II and begin.

Thinks: I could begin *onceupona* or *manyyearsago* or *inadistantcountry*. It's been done. I don't like it.

Or a spot of Calvino clutter – no matter how meticulously brilliant – as if some gabmouth has found a defenceless alienist and vacant couch and is determined, the nerd, to fill the poor bastard in on every nuance of landscape, movement, his reactions thereto, oh God, those endless reactions and possibilities of reactions, and of possibilities of possibilities like some never-ending sorites.

He's lost control!

How about 'Johannes Brahms had a tongue like an adder' or 'John Ruskin loved little girls' or 'Madame Blavatsky's face was deeply pitted with smallpox'? (You looked harder, did you? You liked that? I got your interest?)

This technological world was putting in a bite. No pun there. It was starting to worry the very pith of her. Perhaps it was because of the business she ran, a small newsagency in a God-forgotten tree-stump of a town halfway to nowhere whose population (two hundred and seventy-four) was tucked for leisure either in the bar of the Legless Lizard or in front of television screens, videos, Internet adult movies or PlayStation games for the kiddies.

You want adult movies? she thought. I'll give you adult movies!

No one was reading any more. Or if they were it was the racing form or the sports section of the day-late Brisbane papers. That was the men. She wasn't too sure about the women. A few regulars still bought their weekly dose of women's magazines but she suspected they bought them for the pictures of royals in peril, fornicating actresses and Hollywood studs.

See, despite her age she knew the terms.

Thinks again: *La distance n'y fait rien; il n'y a que le premier pas qui coûte.* So said Madame (marquise, forsooth!) du Deffand in the mid-seventeenth century on hearing Cardinal Polignac describe St Denys' two-mile walk after being beheaded. Let's paraphrase the marquise's words: the length of a book is nothing; it's only the first step that counts. Or the first sentence. Or the first word.

It's that first word.

One must be careful. One must remember what Tennyson said of Patmore: 'Some of his lines seemed hammered out of old nails.'

There are no nails new under the sun. Therefore . . .

It hadn't taken much for her to make a decision.

5

Once upon a ... day ... month ... year ... mountain top ... coral beach ...

Settle for claypan, arid plain, perhaps, a flattish hinterland with gauzy distances where the low Divide moves ever backwards as you chase the paddock grasses, wire fences, switching from verdure to an ochreous sheep-munch.

This will be a book for the world's last reader, she decided, chewing pen-end over an open exercise book. An easy, accessible script with notions formed from those twenty-six black symbols that induce tears or laughter. The miracle of it! Flyspecks on white that can change ideologies or governments, induce wars, starvation, or rare blessings. The very notion brought a rush of excitement and she found herself writing slowly and beautifully 'This will be a book for ...' and stopped because her own emotion was too pretentious for words.

What had decided her? Was it the failure of the tempting stock she had displayed in those first business years, an innocent retired from managing a bookstore in a southern city, translated to late marriage with a farmer who died within four years and left her to sell the farm and work out some life pattern? She could have moved away, but the sale of the farm dragged on for a year and she was interested in exploring the notion of work in a small community rather than the anonymous quality of town. More, she was fifty-plus, relict of a union that had surprised her and her few city friends as a step into the

6

dark. What either of them had wanted was a question that still puzzled: a chance meeting on a Manly ferry, a few laughs, a fish dinner and a what-the-hell feeling about the whole business.

She took over the agency lease on impulse and following old habits stocked the shelves with titles recommended by the *TLS*, the *New York Times Review of Books* and 'little' magazines. (Some crazy dame!) No one had been tempted. There were complaints when she ran out of 'men's' magazines, the bosom-thigh buskers, the car and gun monthlies. She submitted with ill grace – she had to live – and kept her folly purchases for herself in the flat upstairs where already after five years of high-minded failure they choked the ranks of her personal library. Glutted!

In any case, she thought, replacing pen with cigarette and blowing her soul towards the ceiling, who the hell could read these days? Not the kids. Only old codgers like herself.

Last week one of the town lads, handsome son of a town elder, home for the weekend from his boarding-school on the coast, had come in to browse. She watched him shuffle the magazines for ten minutes then went over and offered help. His surprised fourteen-year-old face stared as she suggested a title. She wrote it down for him. He'd examined the piece of paper as if it were Sanskrit.

'Geez, Mrs D, what's that funny stuff you got there?'

'Writing.' She should have been amused. 'I think I write a pretty fair hand.'

'Can't read running writing.'

'What can you read, Toff?'

He gave her a crooked smile. 'I guess things have changed since your day.'

'You still haven't answered me.'

'Printing, man. Like type. Got my own PC and we use them all the time at school.'

'I see. And will you be able to answer exam questions with them come November? Are you all wired up in the examination room, son, so you can type out your essays?'

'No exams for a while. Not public. Anyway, we don't have essays or stuff like that. Just tick boxes.'

'Oh! So you discuss the beauty of the Bard or Mr Eliot by ticking boxes?' (She couldn't help herself.)

Toff was becoming resentful. After all, his daddy was shire president and the wealthiest man in town. 'Don't know what you're talking about.'

'I bet you don't!' she snapped, not caring what his old man thought. She was on the council as well and the pair of them bickered at every meeting. 'I take it you can sign your name in that funny stuff you can't read. Or do you print it or simply put an X?'

The kid raised his eyes to hers in a languidly calculating way and let his glance run down and up the tubby figure in front of him with a terrible calm.

8

'Oh piss off!' he said.

Everything dominated by smart-arse technology, a blurred world of technobuzz. Smack a button for the Library of Congress and home in on your favourite litterer littérateur. Any time, any how. But so hard to read in bed with a weighty computer on your chest. None of that lounging propped on one elbow in the lamplight with moths or rain drumming while you sniffed the delicious scent of paper and binder's glue and the whiff, the very ghost, of printer's ink, the words you wanted to reread coming back as you lazily flicked a page with your finger. Late at night. And the rain. But of course here there was little rain. Perhaps this was a reason for a lost joy. A world full of people, she envisaged, glaring at a screen that glared glassily back.

'Oh God,' she said aloud at the horror of it, lighting another cigarette soother. The smoke curled up and scrawled grey serifs across the air of her upstairs flat, drifting through bedroom, kitchen, bathroom and out to the backstairs landing.

It was an unpretentious place, for she had never been harried by the glamour of any possessions but books. They were everywhere within the few rooms, had taken on colonising attitudes of their own and squatted on chairs, tables, dressers, slumped in ranks along the skirting boards. Many had been purchased in what she now regarded as her personal dreamtime, the student days when she wanted to share with others the joy the books gave her. There were dozens bought cheap from remainder lists, bargains from the slow sellers at the store she had run for nearly twenty years in a side lane off William Street. Ted, she remembered with a blink and a smile, had been aghast at the number of boxes the carrier had brought up from Brisbane, and even more aghast at the contents. 'Where will we put 'em all, love?' Had he expected trousseau sheets? And then there was the residue of mistaken marketing in this townlet, a pile of one hundred or so non-sellers that had made no journeys into outlying farms but had been lugged upstairs to cheer her evenings.

Yes. She guessed he had expected sheets.

At a not quite doddering age but with the irony still running through her veins she would write a book that embraced the themes a lifetime of reading had informed her readers might expect: a narrative line that trolled the waters of sex, suspense, history, tears, laughter. Could she do this? Could she achieve the voice of the times when all her emotional experience was rooted in a convention-riddled past?

No one read. Everyone watched: farragos of smut and violence, sexual thumpings, thumpings of hate and domination, the sanctified brutality of war, the turn-a-blind-eye indifference towards the weak; the fat-bellied, narrow-arsed arrogance of political freaks who made rules for everyone except themselves.

She put down her pen and ran both hands through her greying hair. She thought of thumbs, fingers, that might trace gently, lasciviously, enviously, cynically, the outlines of bodies, contoured clothes, the coiffures of starlets, princesses, rock singers. All in this sapless weather, the January sun hard above the chattering iron roofs under a leaden-blue sky – 'All in the blue unclouded weather . . .'

Well, she had her poetic memory-snippets to keep her warm. Yet there was nothing about her that could make a chapter in her book. Not even a paragraph. Her unoriginality was staggering.

She could barely recall the libidinous years when she had given knockbacks to ginger salesmen armed with all the in-your-face impudence of the seventies, men who became, when she thought of them, another species altogether, alien to the feminine worth she had been reared to believe in. Even to recall maddened.

Life had given no warning that she would end up in a dead town flogging day-late tabloids, boxed games, toys, stationery, greeting cards. The toys grew old. The kids played Nintendo from the moment they discovered the magic of pressing a button. The greeting cards yellowed. She had dumped most of the stock the previous owner displayed and bought French impressionist prints merely to escape the juvenile scatology of the nudge-wink birthday wishes. Now the French impressionists were faded and she had succumbed to the unuttered demands of local taste. Maybe, she thought, walking over to the window and peering into the darkening main street with the Legless Lizard's drunken blaze, the vulgarities should be part of the scheme. Why had she stayed? Was it the memory of Ted?

She turned away and busied herself in the kitchenette, making a sandwich and a pot of tea. The words, she knew, as she sat there with her supper, would be as heavy as bricks when what she wanted to build was some peopled landscape of mist and air. Which could be sharp and heavy as brick. Was that what she wanted? 'Words are more malleable than that,' she said aloud, sipping her tea and staring at the dead night in Drylands. Their definitions were fragile and subject to tides, to misconceptions that insist on clinging.

Take 'clinging', for example.

She pulled a scrap of paper across and wrote down instant suggestions: 'job, town, sick, silk, skin, hands, caring, apathy, belief'. A pretty porridge.

Distressingly, unexpectedly, she recalled the two occasions she had been in love. Once she had been taken to a musical in Brisbane, a stage show called *Lilac Time*.

Schubert. She was twelve. She remained in love for the rest of her life while his music, so agonisingly poised between grief and joy, coloured her mind. That is how I would like to write, she decided. So poised, walking the tightrope between the wet eye, the upcurled mouth. 'You are the rain on my face,' she had thought at twelve, and then written. Then said, 'The clear water over pebbles, the curtain wind-curve of ivy on a wall, a first taste of snow.' Ephemera. She was too young to apply the possibilities of metaphor.

And the second time, ten years older now.

'Whores later,' he had said, smugly urbane. He failed her physically. She persisted. 'Charted your coast without once touching land,' she wrote. 'Land would have me drowned.' '. . . found sea to be safer, sea between the islands.' She wrote and wrote. '. . . guessed at, rather, the inland gentleness beyond the peaks scaled at a first assault.' She wrote. '. . . the tender miles, grass-warm with summer.' And she wrote. '. . . my thin white feet exploratory and tentative as . . . as . . . smiles.'

The pretentiousness of it!

'Ah piss off!' she too had said after a year's frustration with the abstraction of words.

Enclosed.

That was rather that.

The easy way out was reading. She believed it was the easy way out. New places, new people, none of the effort. She became an armchair socialiser and traveller. Her workmates regarded her as eccentric. She retained, still, a sturdy handsomeness, and the blaze of her blue eyes regarded the world with what seemed a casual indifference but in reality computed the tiniest details. She became a watcher rather than participant, so it was almost admission of defeat when she decided to accept Ted's suggestion of marriage. I needed a change, she told herself later. It was time.

She had driven south to Sydney from Brisbane that Christmas into a world of bookshops ripe for harvest and spent five of her seven days' leave stocking up and making orders. On the sixth she took a ferry across the harbour to her fate. 'Drive back with me,' she suggested kindly to Ted over the fish and chips. He turned in his bus ticket the next day and together they set off along the highway, stunned by their impulsiveness. 'The novel,' Lawrence had written – and he had sometimes written a lot of twaddle, she thought sourly, pouring herself a second cup – 'is a great discovery.' Well, yes. He was on target there. She travelled those miles all those years away along the coast road from Sydney to Brisbane. It was when they had stopped for a coffee at a gas station and she was thumbing through a copy of *Phoenix* and grinning in a pleased way at D. H.'s comments on the 'serious' novel while the pump boy filled up the tank that some unknown lout from nowhere sprang into the driver's seat where she had maudlinly left the car keys and driven off leaving a haemorrhage of petrol and a sniggering garage hand.

The police found her car abandoned in the next town, thirty miles north, saved by the weight of reading matter on the back seat. Their suitcases had been opened, scrabbled through and left. The car radio had been neatly extracted but not a book removed.

Now she got up from her seat at the table and hunted along the shelves until she found *A Selection from Phoenix* and prowled through its pages until she came to those terrifying words: '. . . the death bed of the serious novel. It is self-consciousness picked into such fine bits that the bits are most of them invisible, and you have to go by smell. Through thousands and thousands of pages.' There was more. He named writers who tore themselves to pieces and stripped their emotions, as he said, to the finest threads until 'you feel you are sewed up inside a wool mattress that is being slowly shaken up, and you are turning to wool along with the rest of the woolliness.'

Now there was a warning! Avoid what the miner's boy called senile precocity!

She typed a title. She typed up an opening sentence.

She stopped, went over to the stove and made herself a fresh pot of tea. Along the main street in the clamorous dark the pub was yowling towards its climactic closing time. After that, she told herself, after the drunks and the trucks have sorted themselves out, you'll think more clearly, won't you? Two cigarettes till closing and then the drop-cloth of night on Drylands, with only the far-off barking of a farm dog ripping the fabric. This was a town to escape to, rot in, vanish in – cut off from other towns by gravel roads and sorghum acres and sheep paddocks.

Or run from!

Why, this was not quite hell and she was in it.

'Use it,' she said aloud, pouring boiling water onto tea leaves. 'Use the place!'

Here could be the sludge of non-event, she feared. Surely the world's last reader would crave narrative, but how seduce an eye and a brain that had fed for the last two decades on the half-second grab of television, the constant flicker-change of colour and shape against a background of formless noise? A story should fester, should spread its attractive bacteria until it absorbed the whole body. Maybe she could fall back on those old standbys the seven deadly sins: pride, covetousness, lust, anger, gluttony, envy, sloth. She translated: hubris, criminal desire, debauchery, rage, greed, malice, torpor. She dumped the idea. She wanted to make each word sufficient in itself – rivers of words or mountains of them or whatever you could call the geography they created.

But she had stopped often enough in towns this size and the short-lived encounters had reminded her of stirring soup – a sluggish mix bubbling briefly, subsiding briefly. She wished suddenly with all her heart that Ted were sitting with his pipe in the next room and that she could ask him what he wanted.

Ted would know. She was certain he would know. She hadn't discovered until the very day they married and he scrawled something indecipherable on a legal document that Ted couldn't read.

A LONG RUN, A GOOD SEASON

My name is not Franzi Massig.

But I go by that name.

Massig: moderate. Fair enough. But is it verb or adjective? Either fits the bill. Forget the umlaut!

Everyone here – and I have been here four years – believes I am Franzi Massig; and in fact, having discovered a small ancestral shrub of unmet relatives whose wheelings and dealings involve me in more than mental fantasy, with the aid of some judicious pruning I am beginning to believe it myself.

This change of nomenclature was thrust upon me, as they say, more or less. Maybe less. Circumstances that will gradually unpeel forced me to assume another identity. Well, not this particular one. That was a jovial brushstroke on my life's little canvas. But a false identity? I had no choice.

Everyone has a choice, you suggest.

Yes. I agree. But there are circumstances, circumstances. There's bigamy, for a start. Criminality. Boredom. Running for one's life. In fact there are any number of reasons for a name change. The trouble is my change is not now spurious, not superficial. It is in the bone. Or rather, the heart's bone. Yes. Don't nag! I know there's no such thing. I pluck a metaphor, a late-blooming sprig of figurative wankery from that ancestral shrub. A persona alteration.

I am or have become Franzi Massig in fact.

Should I now say 'Once upon a time' or 'There was once' or 'Long ago it happened that'?

I can say that years before the change I happened to read an interesting book called *Another Man's Island*. In French. Perhaps that's where it all began. Perhaps I rationalised my need for a change. Anyway, see me, a computer-wise law firm accountant who stumbled on conspiracy, bribes, pay-offs, drug deals, vast launderings of trust funds in Pacific and Caribbean isles (Ah, the sheer romance of it!) in the most respectable of establishments.

Let's pick that last circumstance I mentioned: running for one's life. Facts and melodrama are commonplace enough. But why me? Me? Me at bay? A dogsbody hacker who was idiotic enough to mention suspicion and unbalanceable ledgers to a senior partner; a hacker who explained how he had tracked pay-offs to police and customs officers and off-shore deposits of corrupt splendour, following a rambler vine of poisonous greenery through leafy acreages of North Shore Sydney to vanishing points in Hong Kong.

Naïvely I had suspected staff corruption at a lower level. Or misplay with the computer.

'You're less than nothing here,' the senior partner told me. 'Keep to what you know.'

I was retrenched that afternoon and returned to my rented post-divorce flat to find it trashed and a threatening note on toilet paper left for me beside the phone.

I'd never been one to argue, not even with my dimming blonde wife who could win any argument with her tongue tied behind her back. I checked into a suburban motel that night and the next day cleaned out my bank account and took a cab to the airport. (This has all the fast-breath trivia of a thriller! You wanted explanation. I shall not refer to these matters again.)

A flight north under an assumed name; the purchase of a second-hand campervan in a south Brisbane car yard known for shady dealings. I stacked the van with food, a small gas cooker, threw out its dubiously stained mattress and substituted a cheap foam lilo. In a bright Brisbane winter afternoon I took it north and then west.

It's big out here, big and pocked with little towns hundreds of yearnings apart, house-clusters that become their own heartland. That's what I sought – anonymity in anonymity.

There was this peak on the western plains, the Virgin Rock, signalling me like a hitcher's thumb after miles of road through sorghum paddocks, the tumbleweed bowling challenges at my fender as I wheeled through dust. But despite the paddocks of fodder, this was no man's land, it would appear, the cultivated *terra nullius* of our founding fathers, a desolation of low hills, and in the last township where I stopped for a sandwich at a greasy spoon the dim hymns of blowflies and the slow decay of the little shops filled me with unspeakable gloom.

Not there. Not there.

I drove on towards a humble lavender range on back roads with the second evening coming down, a glassy tension in the breast, and unexpectedly I found it. A funk-hole! Entrenched! Gone to earth!

There was a piece of land trash, a humpy falling apart in a gidgee clump of forest fringe that kept testing the waters of a creek that ran beside the road. The knockabout town itself was three cooees away. I pulled the van onto the shoulder and went down to the creek that ambled sandily along to lose itself, I discovered later, in the central plains. But now, having filled my water bottles and splashed back through the shallows, I looked up to the far

24

bank to see the late afternoon sun sketch part of a tin roof crouching in the trees and light a diamond sliver of window. I slopped my way to the van and thought about this. I smoked a cigarette. No traffic came along the road. There wasn't even the sound of voices or dog protest.

Something decided me. I backed the van down the road to the log bridge I had only half noticed as I drove, rumbled across and nosed the van up a track no more than a suggestion until I came to the screen of gidgee.

It was here I had detected the giveaway shine on tin, the star flash of glass.

A roof, a floor, studs still in position and timber siding gapped on one wall only. Three rooms – a palace of a place! A listing water tank loud with frog life and a tap connected to shove its snout inside the shack where it dripped over a brimming tin dish that had watered the floorboards for years. Cobwebs spun probabilities across rafters, knitted themselves into corner maps of places where I might like to hide and barricaded with sticky silk an open back door that revealed a track leading to the dunny. I investigated – a plank slung across a cesspit.

Everything! My God, the place had everything!

Here's an aphorism – or is it a paradox? I have always believed not in chance but in the uncanny certainty of coincidence. Let me illustrate:

Tucked away from sight with my van, cloistered in scrub and not even the distant clink of a cowbell or the excited yap of a nosey dog, I inspected my new funk-hole with eagerness. Apart from a crippled table, two chairs (bushman style) and, in the second room (the boudoir), a box bed with wire mattress, a leprous mirror hanging from a nail and a chest of drawers preserving the detritus of washed-up settlers, there were a couple of kerosene lamps, a rusting primus and an assortment of empty canisters. The paucity of what was left behind had the melancholic harmonics of wistful music.

Someone had poured this concrete floor in a hurry. Whoever it was had used too much sand, insufficient cement. Large areas were crumbling and the dank pieces of matting that hid the rougher spots had the sadness of house-proud optimism. Wherever I looked – through open door, window – there was nothing but a green camouflage that suited me. Had it suited whoever was here before? Behind the back door a stiffened tea-towel hung. I pulled its cardboard pleats apart and found a greeting in German, *'guten Morgen, guten Abend'*, spelled out below; above, an impossible Rhine castle, and in the right-hand corner the shadowy words *Heidelberg, a view of the Neckar*. Sad. Sad.

A rural slum. A camp-site. A dream of a hideaway.

Pushing my way back to the van through swags of scrub, gorging on invisibility, I fetched my thermos and took it over to the shack for a baptismal session, libation, whatever. Distantly, a cow lowed, a dog barked, and then the silence of leaves and insects.

In the bedroom I began an unchivalrous rootling through the chest of drawers, poking about in a jetsam of hair pins, bills, letters, bits of ribbon, a bible, a hairbrush still clinging to long red hairs, and dust. Always dust. Above, in the muddied mirror, the previous owner, glimpsed through swirls of cloud and fog, watched me finger these wretched leavings, smiling forgivingly as I stretched a fine auburn hair to its gleaming twenty-inch length.

Despite exhaustion and a niggling fear of uncovery both here and back there, always the curious opportunist, I took the letters and postcards to the van, heated more coffee on the primus and settled down to track fragments of a life other than mine.

The letters were few and had been stuffed back in envelopes that bore, I observed, a faded Deutschland postmark. I felt guilty opening them. I stuffed the guilt back in my envelope self.

Dearest Gerda (began the first I pulled out, dated October '78, Heidelberg), *I wish I was with you in the sensual zones! It's very cold here – both climate and hospitality are freezing me out. I don't think my long-lost just-met uncle and aunt really want to have a rough-hewn colonial stranger thrust on them, despite the blood connection. And my German isn't really up to it. I've forgotten almost everything I*

*learnt as a kid. My father's brother looks at me –
suspiciously might be the word – as if he doubts my
claims to being family. I dangle all my father's intimate keepsakes as proof: snapshots showing both of
them, for heaven's sake, birth certificate, and so on,
but even then Uncle Gustave's eyes flicker. As I say, I
have little German and his and Aunt Liese's English is
basic. I think he thinks I'm a fraud.*

*So all being well I won't be staying long. After all,
it was only an exercise in nostalgia, which is a short-
lived fever at the best.* (I must say I like his writing
style.) *I gave him the letter Father wrote before he
died and the watch he wanted him to have – appar-
ently it was a watch Uncle treasured as a kid – and the
old beggar hrumped and ha'd over them both, not
telling me what the letter said. But I heard him and
Aunt Liese talking long into the night, arguing, it
sounded like. Huh! So I'll be home by Christmas,
perhaps earlier. That's just a few weeks away. All
my love.*

    Carl

I drank my coffee, my mouth burning on the cup rim,
and put the letter carefully back into its envelope. If I were
Carl, I tried to imagine, and not this refugee from corpo-
rate revenge, a whistle-blower on the run, what then?

The next letter I opened was dated a week later. Why

had Gerda kept them? More to the point, why had she left them behind?

My cousin Franzi is a nice fellow, only about twenty-five but as he is completely fluent in English he acts as interpreter between me and my dear relatives. He's some kind of tutor or research fellow at the university, is completing a doctorate and is the apple of Uncle Gustave's bleak eye – a narrow and doubting one of the lightest blue.

(Had Carl returned as promised?

There wasn't a shred of plastic holly, mistletoe, fir-tree glitter. In the corners of each drawer were fluff balls and dead insects. That was all that was left of a relationship, was it? Poor Gerda! Or am I wrong? Hairs on a brush, forgotten letters, small mounds of clutter.)

Uncle Gustave has a puckered scar running from the corner of his left eyebrow to the southern beach of his mouth. 'La guerre,' he explains – we get by occasionally in schoolroom French – and for the moment I am horrified at how the righteous (that's us!) inflicted pain as well on pawns who possibly cared nothing at all for the political lusts of their leaders. 'I had eighteen years,' he tells me, resorting to his rotten English and translating direct from his rotten French. 'Only

29

eighteen years. And then this.' Fifty-six years, Uncle has, and the bitterness of all scars remains. Especially that of my father's escape across the borders to evade the coming war. He can't forgive Dad's desertion on the eve of Armageddon. Traitor to the Fatherland, he calls him. So Franzi tells me.

Franzi is a cheerful fellow, not like his father. We have fun together. Some days we walk up to the university to meet his friends, over a big sort of bridge to the marvellous old buildings, or we go down to the Hauptstrasse for a meal. Meals are so huge there is something gross about them, and even the cleanliness, the cleanliness, the cleanliness. We sit in the summer-house in the gardens above the Neckar where Speer is supposed to have met Hitler and none of all that horror seems believable. None of it.

'One day,' Franzi tells me, 'I'll visit your country. Stay maybe.' 'We'll welcome you,' I tell him. And we will, won't we, Gerda?

I'm writing this in that very summer-house where Albert Speer planned tactics. So will I. In this cold air I cannot feel the ghostly footprints.

I've made a decision. I'm leaving in three days. Blessings and

The next page was missing.

I suspect he never did leave Germany and I imagine,

in my fevered excitement at having discovered my own fastness isolated enough to conceal, that Gerda – his wife? partner? – fed up with his absence and the burden of solitary child care (there was a broken plastic rattle under the bed) in such a primitive place, finally gathered up her possessions and left, baby clutched to the breast as a talisman of a lost relationship.

But I could be wrong.

The tank water stinks.

I spit again and again the vestiges of my testing sip and go down to the creek with my water bottle and ponder the set-up while the primus heats up the kettle. Just for the moment I'm prepared to camp illegally. Maybe tomorrow I can talk business with the owner of that farm whose roof I saw beyond the scrub. In the meantime the primus pants busily and I spoon more generous measures of coffee into my pot and sit back on my bunk assessing.

Here I am in a natural cavern created by gidgee and eucalypt, the van backed up against a cluster of tough-trunked stringybarks, its nose poised for flight. But will there be need? I'm over-dramatising. Now there's the distant yelping of a dog, and later, in an after-dark sortie, I get a look at the farm and shed whose roof, a mile up the slope, had warned me with its sunset blaze of possible trespass.

This is no man's land as well, I hope, or that of an obliging farmer. A few days before, I had almost settled for the desolation of hills and abandoned mullock heaps and poppet heads in an old mining town north of here. Cages and tanks had long been dismantled and left to rust on abandoned leases treacherous with barbwire slung around the shaft openings and wrecks of machinery at which grass licked with stringy yellow tongues.

I stopped there too in that decaying township for a cup of tea at the one general store. Graveyard music. A dozen cottages, drunk with summer, straggled along the main street, the only street. The tea-break was a mistake. It excited curiosity. A few old men watched me from the pub verandah and one of them ('Can I help you, mate?') sauntered over for an explanation of my presence. I abandoned that brown and yellow hillside on the casual wheels of tossed lies that insisted – but breezily – that I was heading east to the coast and north for the cape and accelerated from ancient interested eyes over tan landscape whose gullies and small streams had almost forgotten the pollution that clogged them.

Yes. It's easier to disappear in a crowd.

But I haven't chosen crowds.

I shall put all this down. It's pretty smart these days,

so my reading tells me, to avoid the narrative line like the plague. Narrative merely packs you in with the cloggers, the airport glossies, thick tomes designed for the eighteen-, the twenty-four-hour flight to another terminal where you'll glimpse, as you stagger cabwards dehumanised from the twice-cooked meals and body cramp and changeovers, pre-fliers fingering the book-stall thickies seeking print oblivion.

Chuck your read tomes into the queues. Watch them leap to take a mark.

Hey! Take a Nembutal!

Where I come from, that's how I could have begun.

And what would you have? A country gawk whose father and his father before him had worked in claypan country just east of Isa, in droughtland that killed off the sheep as fast as they put them there? When I wasn't at school in the Taws, I was back home helping Father kill the sheep that were dying from lack of feed, lack of water, bogged in the sticky glue of drying waterholes.

My parents sold up, eventually, God knows how, and took the residue of the sale to an outer suburb north of Brisbane where they could keep in touch with sonny-boy who was completing an accountancy course at a technical college.

'I can't bear the suburbs,' Mother said, Father said. After thirty years on twenty thousand acres, how could they? Settling for a green five-acre lot near the Glasshouse

33

Mountains was better than nothing, I suppose, and I watched them take to gardening like obsessives. A creek from which they pumped cut the rear corners of the block and they planted exotics that they had never been able to cultivate out west. Within three years I could lose sight of the old loves fifty feet from the house, as they were to lose sight of me when I went south to Sydney, bristling with high distinctions, to work for a legal firm.

God, I should have been bored!

Merely writing the above I feel the stasis of a yawn begin its upward surge. Caaaaaaaw!

Perhaps it was meanness of spirit, an ungenerosity, envy — whatever — that had started me on an I-spy investigation of privileged boss funds. I could claim it was a fanatical probity drummed in from an early age by Calvinist parents who had not once attempted curly bowling at tax-men, bankers, creditors. I could claim that. Maybe it was a sheer desire to see the balancing of ledgers, the beautiful equation between losses and profits making X equal Y. Yes. Look, it was that – the Calvinist equation. And I longed to see it as if it were the Grail. When my failure to find even the dimmest shape of that glimmering icon unearthed only malfeasance, irritation won. I reported the misplay that denied me the golden gleam.

Ergo . . .

No. I didn't personally want the Caymans, the Virgin Isles, Vanuatu, Majorca – those paradises of non-taxable venality. I wanted this land with its shallow Calvinist dish of red dust and claypan.

My parents died a year before this crisis, killed in a joy flight over Moreton Bay. Their five acres and house that had been hidden eventually under plaited leaves was sold up to a refugee from the city and I had been left with a smallish inheritance sitting in a credit union. I could flee, I could be self-supporting for a few years. Was I exaggerating the menace I felt? Certainly my actions in exposing graft and embezzlement had resulted by the end of a month in a series of newspaper articles and charges being laid. (I'm a bit of a gabmouth. I had journalist buddies.) I'm looking ahead at this point. So little that is punishable in any ethical society is punished in this one. It would all blow over for the senior partners. Nothing would have to be repaid. Boss nest-eggs, weekenders, luxury cars and numbered bank accounts in faraway places would be safe. There was only the small surf of scandal to ride out, and even being struck off the legal rolls was a mere hiccup, the post-port belch people like Tyrannosaurus Lex had been emitting during decades of business lunches.

Skip the lunches.

The unforgiven unforgivable one was me. The

whistle-blower. Pursuit of that piece of righteousness could go on for the rest of my life. That's how it works here.

All together, now, sing, in high falsetto, those words of our dear old anthem: Our land is rort by sea!

Changing identity is a tricky business.

A false licence is an Open Sesame to escape routes.

I drove away from my camp-site beside the creek and headed back to the coast, crossing the Tropic and moving north to hole up in a cheap pub in Townsville and take driving lessons.

'Name?' asked the pert teenager behind the desk of the driving school.

'Massig,' I said. 'Franzi Massig.' She bit her pen with alarm. 'Here. Let me.' I reached over and filled in the form.

'That's a funny name,' she said.

'Yes, isn't it! German.'

'Oh,' she said.

'I came out when I was five. My parents were migrants. My father worked on the Snowy scheme.'

'What's that?' she asked.

'Never mind,' I said. 'What's a pretty girl like you doing worrying about things lost in the mists of time?'

That brought a smile. This was hard work.

'ID?'

'Look,' I said, 'I'm up here on a working holiday and eventually I'll need to rent a car. I didn't know I'd need a birth certificate.'

She smiled again. 'Well, credit cards?'

'I always pay cash,' I said, producing cash. Another apple. Another Eden.

'Oh well,' she said.

'Thank you. I am most obliged.' We swapped smiles.

After that, it was remarkably smooth sailing, especially when I urged my driving teacher who, incidentally, was amazed by my rapidly acquired expertise at the wheel, to call me Frank. He could come to grips with a name like that.

That's the trouble with everything these days. The effects of technology. You have to be listed on a computer somewhere, somehow, get wired before anyone will concede you exist.

I abandoned the van in a shopping-centre car park somewhere in Bundaberg and rode a bus back up the coast. There was a terrible amount of to-ing and fro-ing as I laid false scents. In Townsville once more I bought another van. I had a new name on my driving licence and registration papers. I opened a new bank account.

Outwardly I acted the part of a breadline Bert. Some sort of low-profile employment was indicated: odd-job man, office cleaner, all-round fixer. I couldn't make up my mind between these intoxicating choices.

Now that I had a name change, now that I had a little money, despite premonitions of discovery that ruffled my sleep and made me stick to back roads, almost automatically I found myself driving south and west once more to the source of my new identity. This time, however, I would enter, trumpets blazing, in a mess of flags.

Having taken co-ordinates, I thought, smirking with trigonometric sheen, estimated time of arrival would be mid-evening.

There are now two hundred and seventy-five people in this town, the late arrival having drifted into the bar of the Legless Lizard, alive with wizened old gaffers escaped from their homes and a loud group of wild boys drinking round the pool table. The manager is also the barman, and the manager's wife the bar-girl. The manager (Clem, I discover later) is a dark-moustached gent dressed far too young for his age and could give his bar-girl wife, who is a blonde and string-thin, a good twenty years. There is something odd about the set-up. He has a creamy deep-south American accent. She has the forceful rasp of a Gold Coast tearaway.

Between the hubbub of orders I book myself a room for a week, to unbelieving looks from the girl-wife and those drinkers close enough to listen in. After dumping my bag in an upstairs room ('No one's staying. Grab yourself a room on the front side. The wife and I have a flat at the back.') I return to the bar for a nightcap and get sociable.

'Come far, mate?' someone asks after a watching while.

'In from the coast,' I say.

'Staying long?'

I consider saying 'Just passing through' but something makes me commit myself. 'Looking for a patch,' I offer. 'Just a small piece of dirt with maybe a creek.' Several voices assure me I'd be lucky and then there are all those dropped queries: Where are you from, mate? What line are you in? And so on. Mate's elated at the glibness of his lies: a broken marriage, he explains, offering reality, a vague 'Back-of-Cairns, forced to sell up with the split, looking for something smaller, the money's dropped out of the tobacco industry.' We take two beers and a lot of cigarettes to discuss what's wrong with the tobacco business and then I plead exhaustion and push my way up the uncarpeted stairs to a twelve-by-eight room opening onto the wide verandah.

The next night I damp down that curiosity by saying how much I like the look of the country hereabouts and, sensing the beginnings of approval, I shout the first round. But weather-eyes are still open. Merv (on my right) and Barney (on my left) tell me I can't go wrong in this neck of the woods. 'You can't go wrong, mate,' they say, affirming words with nods. 'Been here twenty years,' Barney says. 'Wouldn't be any place else.'

Twenty years? I'm doing sums before dropping my first important lie. 'And what you say your name was?' Barney asks.

'Massig. Frank Massig. My friends call me Franzi.'

'That'd be German, eh?' Barney says. 'There was a young bloke with a name like that when I first come up here shearing. Renting out of town, he was. Bit of a hippie like but not a bad sort of bloke. Buggered off suddenly, him and his missus. Well, he went first and she must of gone soon after.'

'That was my cousin,' I explain, gallant and excusing. 'He went back south. His dad died on the Snowy scheme. He's still down that way as far as I know. Carl. Used to talk so much about up here when I saw him last. That would be easily five years back though, and we've lost touch. Still, I remembered all the things he used to say about the place, so when things went wrong for me up north I had to come and see for myself.'

'So you're German, too,' Merv says, pressing the point. He's a squat, solid man with a broken nose and killer thumbs. But his mouth's kind. There's a good-natured curve.

'Australian,' I say, deliberately tightening my lips. 'My parents migrated in '50 and I was born here. Mother

40

was an English girl nursing in Europe when she met Dad. He was a bit of a mess. Shot down, you know.'

This is easy: the full flight of the burgeoning untruth. Suddenly I remember telling the driver school secretary I came out at five. Never mind. I'll stick with this one. I find I can improvise like an old jazz maestro, piling up riffs and breakaway cadenzas. 'Badly scarred from burns. Look, everyone suffered. No hard feelings, eh?'

Barney lights up, drags in smoke and expels slowly. 'That's right, mate. We all suffered. Me and Merv, we were stuck up in New Guinea. Them bloody Japs were worse than any German, I'd say. Anyway, you're half a Brit. That's the main thing.'

'Yeah,' Merv agrees. 'That's the main thing.' He grins suddenly. 'I'll get the next round.'

I breathe in the pub: there's the unremovable stench of stale beer and smoke. Forty years back, maybe, the tongue and groove walls had been painted white. It's a yellow memory. At one end of the bar a door to the hallway and office. At the other end of the bar, next to the dartboard and the pool table, a door opens onto a side lane. Across the hallway there's a ladies' lounge with no one in it. Staff? There seems to be only the pub owner and his partner, who looks disgruntled and deals short-temperedly with the younger men who huddle away from the plastic choppers, the hairy ears, the beer guts. The television screeches above everybody.

At the risk of alienating Merv and Barney I am tempted to ask for a pina colada. (Just checking!) I ask. 'Certainly, sir,' the pub owner says, unblinking, and in three minutes flat there's a frothy yellow concoction in a brandy balloon. I don't believe this.

'Jesus!' Barney says. 'What's that pansy stuff?'

Do I detect the lingering twist of smile lurking under Clem's moustache?

Keep a low profile. Agree. Melt in. Be dull, conservative and so orthodox the town forgets you are there. Treat the drink as a bit of a joke. Never do that again.

If I had been an adequate chess player I would never make cultural mis-steps like that. There's a flippancy I can't control.

A background. I must flesh out a background that doesn't waver. Before I again settle into sleep in that upstairs room whose iron-frame bed has a quilt of the kind my grandmother used, I sort lies like a well-loved, well-thumbed pack of cards. I try them out, my face mumbling into the pillow. Ordinariness is all.

I consider the lies already told. Should I flesh them out further? Forget that mythical wife abandoned on the Atherton Tableland and offer data about the real one who abandoned me? ('Mate, I don't want to talk about it. Okay? Still hurts.') Would that be too easy to check out?

Boringly, grindingly reasonable is the aim. Coming as a stranger into a no-count hick town at the back of nowhere and wanting to settle is stretching the disinterest of country folk. But before the north? These tiny communities demand knowledge of before. How about, I ask myself on the lip of sleep, a small convenience store in the hills out-side Adelaide? Now, I like that. Could account for the name, the background after the Snowy. Lot of German set-tlers there. I develop the lie and retire Dad from the Snowy to place his accumulated savings in this smallgoods shop: liverwurst, bratwurst. The wurst is yet to be. I grin into the lumpy pillow. Helped out with my parents until their mixed goods was killed off by the supermarkets. Anyway, I wanted a change, a bit of a rest. But still wanted country, small towns. Used to that. Used to . . . sleep.

My problem is remembering the lies.

Now four years on and accepted.

(He hoped. He was beginning to think of himself in the third person.

At least they were accustomed to his presence. But he was still a newcomer. Even after four years.)

A bar-room introduction to Jim Randler and I had

43

obtained a lease with an agreement to purchase on that small ten-acre patch by the creek. For the first year I worked as yardman and bar-useful two nights a week at the pub, and watched Clem and Joss cope with drunks and rednecks with the chilling aplomb I had first noticed.

I felt safe. I had almost forgotten the reasons that brought me here and answered readily to my new name. Old Randler on the farm back of me had asked a few searching questions during the preliminaries of rent-lease-purchase. He had known my cousin Carl briefly, he told me, and found him an aloof character with few practical skills who seemed disinclined to accept advice or even help.

'Now, that little wife he had with him,' old Randler said, settling down to a cuppa and a pipe on his verandah, 'she was a different matter. I felt sorry for her. She tried so hard for the few months they were here to make a go of it. Little bits and pieces, you know what women are like.' I thought of the heap of grimy curtains and bedding I would lug outside and burn, eager to destroy any evidence I might have missed. 'Then the bugger vanished overnight. She said he'd gone back to Germany to do something for his dad.'

'That's right,' I agreed. I nearly added that that was when we had met but remembered in time that I'd been born out here and hadn't seen my cousin for years. Mr Randler noted my munched openers and pause.

'Yes?' A curious grey glance. He looked me in the eye. 'I think the poor kid was pregnant. Not that she said anything to me, mind you. But she seemed pretty miserable that last week. Said he was coming back for Christmas. And then one morning in the new year she was gone too. Someone saw her take the mail train out to the coast.'

He added, as much for himself as for me, that the place was a bit of a mess. Together we inspected it as if I'd never seen it before and he made offers of help with tanks and plumbing. Where was Mrs Randler? I shied at asking and he volunteered nothing at that first meeting, but I nosed about in town to learn that he'd always been tied to helping his old man. Some of those diehard settlers had feudal views. I refrained from comment.

The place should really have been burnt down but I persevered with patching, in between odd-jobbing for the Legless Lizard. Gradually the shack took on a neater and cleaner appearance. I hacked out spaces for windows and installed a water closet in the dunny shed. As I said before – everything!

For years. Four years.

Things have changed. Are changing.

A week ago I found Clem cuddling a tearful Joss in the kitchen, holding and rocking her like a baby. Next day Joss had gone. I wait for Clem to tell me. He doesn't. Not really. 'We're thinking of moving on,' he says. 'Joss has gone ahead to look around.'

And I feel lately that I am being watched.

There's nothing concrete about this, just the sense of eyes, eyes that crawl across the back of my neck. When I swing around – nothing. Simply Clem washing the glasses, spreading the bar towels, emptying ashtrays. I've gone quickly to the street door but there is only the distant figure of someone walking away on the other side of the road, usually a local I know. (Hi, Bert! Cheers, Darkie!) Twice it has been a stranger, back view only, hat brim down, opening up his four-wheel drive and getting in to push out along the main drag and take the inland road. There's nothing unusual about this. Lately our town has been a source of interest to tourists and fossickers. There have been traces of gemstone on the northern face of the Rock. The town is divided on the matter: the council wants tourism, that cheap bastard industry, but it wants to preserve Drylands' only attraction, the weird escarpment that, at certain hours of the day, in certain angles of sun and shadow, creates an illusion of the Madonna and child that lasts several minutes. Geez, mate! Cop that, eh!

Perhaps Clem is watching. He has no reason. Joss and I had a working relationship of chiack and cheer.

46

I'd tarted up the ladies' lounge with potted plants and once a week on Friday evenings, our busiest time, had tossed up a counter meal in the kitchen. Simple stuff: chops and veg, steak and veg. The customers ate with eyes glued to the sports channel, hands moving forks automatically to gaping mouths.

I watched the eaters. There was Howie Briceland wolfing sausage and mash with Fred Cunneen. In the ladies' lounge Mrs Locke picked delicately, as she did each Friday evening, at a singed cutlet with Janet Deakin from the newsagency. I'm the watcher.

Yet take yesterday.

I drove home after the evening shift at the Lizard to find the shack tingling with the aftermath of intrusion. No one locks up here. My few possessions had been slightly moved around, books replaced out of order on shelves, underwear tossed about, some microscopic realignments to the geometry of crockery placements.

Yes, it's years since I worried about reprisals from my old firm in some lurid fiction scenario – and yes, I've grown a beard, a neat torpedo with clipped moustache, the whole affair grey-streaked by now and making me another man altogether from the idiot runner of four years ago. I fit into this place. I'm part of its smallness even if the whole town thinks of me as a blow-in.

But beside the shiftings, the fumblings, the sortings,

there was a hand-printed note left on my pillow: *Who the hell do you think you are?*

Now, that's a philosophic question.

Clem, absent-minded but addicted to customer pleasings, has the bar television tuned to the idiot screeches and howlings of an in-your-face teen programme, *The Groin Busters*. For God's sake!

'Only till the sport comes on.'

'I don't know whether I can stand it. It's withering my mind.'

'That's what it's meant to do. That's why the country's full of mindless shits. Only five more minutes, Frank. The old hands don't notice. They're brain-drained by the young. It's the same in the States. Haven't a protest left between them. If I don't leave it on I'll forget to tune in and they'll miss the start of the game.'

Yes. That's the way it is out here. Even if the underage cannot drink at the pub, they hang about outside swigging cola and smoke defiantly, letting their great lugs linger at open doorways so as not to miss one nuance (there's *no* nuance) of the din ripping the street wide open.

The open door exposes a newcomer, well, hardly new – a tall, middle-aged, jeans-clad loiterer who is watching as I wipe down tables, change drink coasters, swab counters. Clem switches off the sound. Before I can approach he's gone, but Clem, pausing between solo passages at the cash register, looks across.

'Do you know that guy?'

'No.'

'He was asking about you?'

'Me? When?'

'Oh, couple of weeks back. Asked your name. Said he thought he knew you. Seemed harmless enough. You weren't about at the time and I forgot to let you know. Sure you haven't seen him before?'

'Quite sure. But lately, I've got to admit, I get this crazy feeling I'm being watched. Creepy.'

'Some dark secret in your past, buddy?' Clem says slyly, making me think he's thinking of Joss, knowing I liked her and hoping for payback, vicariously of course. Three years back a contract killer moved into town for a couple of months. Well, that was the story. The local copper from Red Plains kept his head down. You'd have liked him, everyone said. Good with kids. Loved animals. He holed up in the Lizard for all that time, only appearing for meals, and was gone as unobtrusively as he'd come. I didn't like to remember that. 'Maybe this feller'll look you up and let you know what it's all about.'

'It can't be about anything,' I say more defensively than is warranted. I slam two chairs back into position and switch on the cleaner. Any further questions from Clem don't have a hope. He responds by switching on the sound system again, so loudly I can feel the vibrations from every wall.

'Jesus, man,' old Jim Randler says, coming in for his one morning beer. 'Can you turn that fuckin thing down!'

Now, Jim Randler knows who he thinks he is. But do I? So many years with the wrong name but the under-me has not changed a whit. I'm still the unaggressive mid-performer from way back, saturated with all those Protestant ethics Ma and Pa drummed in from dummy-time. The cause of my downfall, of course, and the reason I'm here. If I weren't, I ponder, back behind the bar and polishing glasses automatically, would I be any happier in the city sprawl of nine-to-five, moving up the accountancy ladder to some grand age of fifty and the sack because a cleaner-cut youth whose daddy drank with the boss was in need of a leg-in?

No. I like it here. Proof of my humdrummery. My shack is in order, my fruit garden battling the seasonal droughts, my income from the Lizard enough to keep me in steaks and a monthly trip away on the coast. Face it, there isn't much else.

The bar begins to fill up, the sports programme roars and I'm busy pulling pints when Clem digs me in the ribs and nods across the room. Shock!

He's come in, that snooper. He's taken a seat by the street window and when he catches my eye lifts one finger in a summoning way I resent. So I take my time going over and he eyeballs me in a quizzical, amused fashion. His order? A schnapps. No schnapps. Well, a schooner then. He has an accent I can't quite place, thick, furry, but the syntax is impeccable. 'New around here?' I ask. 'Just looking around,' he says, but looking at me hard. Inspecting – head to shoes and back again.

Clem says later, during a break in the morning session when the old hands wander off for lunch with kitchen-aggrieved wives, 'Find out anything?' I shake my head and help myself to a handful of free peanuts from a bar bowl. 'You know, he was asking one of the shearers last week where you lived.'

Well, I can't say I like the sound of that. My imposture, which at times I totally forget as a pardonable venial offence, occasionally hits me as more than a romantic fabrication, as more than the disguise I decided was necessary four years back. The whole set-up shivers with legal retribution in all senses. I eat a gloomy lunch in the kitchen, recalling those sharp and challenging blue eyes whose stare has disrupted my equanimity.

That night I bolted my doors but still slept fitfully, waking at every animal crash or thud in the darkness of the scrub by the creek. Once, I saw the flash of a torch beyond the treeline – it was after two – and although I

51

waited for the crackle of twig, the pad of footsteps to follow, there was nothing.

I lay awake till dawn.

'I'd like a weekend off,' I told Clem the next morning. 'I'd like to head down the coast for a few days. Can you get someone to fill in?'

'Sure,' Clem agreed easily. 'Enjoy.'

Why do people come to places like this?

Is it the loneliness in themselves seeking an outer evidence of the solitary? Is it the belief that in such a small town they will find the corrosive for their solipsist attitudes, that they'll be taken in all warm-kissy-huggy? Drinking mates? The best of old buggers?

No way.

Back in the shack I pack a bag, take my fishing lines and head out to the campervan. We're old mates now and I sink into the driving seat with a second sense of escape, to drive without knowing I'm driving, going over the past weeks, recalling Clem eyeing me oddly only two days ago and saying, 'You know, Franzi, that feller looking for you could be a brother. Haven't you noticed? Same colouring, same features. He's even got the beard.'

I'd gone back to the washroom and examined myself in the mirror. Blue-eyed, greying blond with a high complexion now heading for effacement behind the side-tags of my torpedo. No. I hadn't noticed. There'd been no start of mirror-image shock when he walked straight towards me once in the main street or when he'd asked for a schnapps. Look, Clem, I mutter as I drive east, even when I see my goddam face unexpectedly in a shop window I don't recognise myself. Why should I? All of us see ourselves as others – the other we wish to be, and sometimes the other we hope not to be. The true, agonising reality is shoved further and further back.

And afterwards? After the three score and ten is done with, the last human smells of sweat, faeces, urine fading, then is the ultimate loneliness, the confrontation with the god figure for eternity. Or maybe it won't be confrontation. Instead of welcoming arms, the eyes will turn away for all time.

The hell with this, I think, and prepare to fish myself stupid at a small beach I've checked out before, a curve of sand and river lagoon where red brick hasn't yet arrived. There's still the old convenience store with its milk and bread and ancient tins of baked beans and tuna and boxes of dying vegetables. The same old bloke is running it. We exchange mundanities on the margins of non-knowing.

Two good days. I don't think of Drylands until halfway on the drive back, a heap of gutted fish packed in ice in the esky. I'm longing for a leisurely late meal.

It's night by the time I reach town, the main street

53

freckled with lights and the doors of the pub wide open to the hot summer evening. I slow as I drive past and see Clem behind the bar, dour, as he works the beer pump. And just over the heads of the drinkers I see his part-time help, my weekend replacement.

God! It's the snooper, the fair-haired busybody who's been in and out of town for the last fortnight. I pull up and sit in the cabin of my van, watching as he takes orders and handles the drinkers with all the panache of an old hand. Is this how I look? Is it? Am I favoured with a deadpan glance at the me of me?

Rage or misgiving? I can't analyse what makes me drive off with a screech of tyres like any lout on wheels and shove the van back down the main strip. I need company. A sympathetic voice.

I park outside the newsagency and sit for a moment until the transparency of my offended vision becomes opaque, then I take the esky and go round the back to the yard stairs.

There's a wait while I hear Janet patter across her living-room to turn down the tapedeck where Bunny Berrigan's trumpet is straining towards the empyrean. He can't get started! What about me?

Silence.

'Hello,' she says, opening the door wide on a room littered with books and paper, and I thrust the esky forward as a sweetener.

I'm calmer already watching her welcome face break into a smile, her eyes amused as she peers into the esky.

'Splendid!' she says. 'Splendid!'

So I go to her kitchenette and help prepare the fillets while she gets a pan going with oil, and the splatter of heated crisping fish brings me back to normal mental temperature and the two of us sit to a late dinner and empty a bottle of white.

Back. Integrated. I feel part of the place again, one of its essential ingredients. I'm on the verge of admission but although Janet is safe and discreet I prefer her to believe I've dropped by from friendship, not need. It's only surface knowledge I have of her. She has less of me. Yet from my first days in this town she has been a steadying warmth at the back of my mind.

It's nearly midnight when I rise to go. The pub has been quiet for over an hour. The main street is glazed with moonlight washing into the yards of shops and houses. Lights are out in the Legless Lizard. The drinkers' cars have gone. There's a simple and terrible honesty about the place that makes it a town with nothing to hide. I drive slowly now, calmly, heading down the road to the turn-off that will take me up the gravel past Randler's house and onto the track that leads down to the creek and my shack.

Even as I swing the van around the last stand of wattle, I see a light from my windows and my heart becomes clamorous in the dark, thudding hard against the walls of my chest. I park the van, giving the door an aggressive slam, and stride angrily up to the shack.

The door is ajar but I fling it wide open and there he is, sitting back insolently at home in my one easychair, sipping from a mug of tea, his eyes inspecting me over an unreadable smile as I crash the door to in rage.

No words, nothing. Beside him on the table I see the opened packet, that wretchedly small packet of letters I had found four years ago and kept out of sentiment.

He taps the packet with one finger but does not take his eyes from my face.

'I am Franzi Massig,' he says.

What will happen now?

MEANWHILE . . .

She opened up the newsagency at seven-thirty and watched Drylands come to life, the early risers driving in for papers, the yardman at the Lizard sweeping down then hosing the pub verandah. There was something about him, she felt, had always felt, that didn't quite fit, but she waved and he waved back.

Behind the counter in the shop she sat waiting for customers as thoughts slipped back and forth – yardman to Ted. She'd hoped for a while that the bar-useful, as he called himself, might be a reader but he seemed interested only in the southern papers, of which the few copies she ordered always came several days late.

'Ted,' she said aloud to the empty shop. Ted could have been a reader, Ted with spectacles slipping down his nose in the after-dinner quiet.

It had had to be done with tact.

Ted was a man who could handle tractor engines with aplomb, was so mechanically literate, with his clever intuitive fingers and quick mind assessing the nub of problems, that she hesitated to put it crudely to him that she could teach him to read.

She began by leaving small notes on the kitchen table when she had to drive over to the shopping mall at Red Plains, simple messages that told him lunch was in the fridge or the time she would be back. He could handle numbers and the very simplest words. She wanted more for him.

'How did it happen, Ted?' she asked one night when they sat comfortable on the back verandah after tea. 'That you missed out on reading?'

She hated herself when she saw the faint pink stain move up his cheeks.

He thought about her question for a long while and then he said, 'I guess it was those first years, really. When I just started. They say they're the most important, don't they? Mum was sick a lot after I was born, my dad told me, and she got worse. We had a place north of Red Plains then and it was Mum's job to drive me in to school, but some mornings she was too sick so I stayed home. Then after she died, I was seven, eight, maybe, it all fell onto the old man and I missed out again, staying home to help in the busy seasons and never catching up.'

'I can help if you like.'

'It's too late, Janet love,' he said.

'It's never too late. Give me a month.'

Ted stirred his tea, embarrassed. 'It wouldn't be worth it. All that trouble, eh? Couldn't put you through that.'

'Give me a month,' she insisted. 'It's worth all the trouble in the world.'

It took more than a month.

For a start there was difficulty obtaining those preparatory school readers that were used in Ted's early years. Finally an old school friend in Brisbane hunted her down a thumbed set and she began, mindful all the time of that male myth that women were more stupid, less acute, had no brains in fact, and that it diminished a man to be shown how to do anything at all by a female.

'You've got to want to do it, Ted,' she warned him. 'Otherwise it's no good.'

'I'll give it a try,' he said, 'just for you.'

She taught him the sounds of the letters. By the end of a fortnight Ted had read his way through the first primer.

'Practise aloud in the lav, Ted,' she advised. 'Then you won't feel silly about it.'

One morning at the start of the third week, she trudged up past the dunny to feed the chooks in the top yard and could hear Ted's voice in the spider gloom of the lavatory reading aloud. '"Sam has a tan hat. Bess has a red cap." That bloody Bess! Just like Janet!' She grinned and half cried as she fed the squawking hens. 'Oh Ted,' she whispered to herself, 'you're on the way.'

She encouraged him to copy the words onto an old pad. She made sure she was out at those times. One day she returned from shopping at Red Plains to find the house empty and the sound of the tractor racketing over the far ten acres. On the refrigerator door Ted had stuck a note: *Your lunch is on the table.*

Victory! Janet ate the sandwich he had cut into neat triangles and cried and cried.

He covered the second reader in another fortnight and she found his old writing pad filled, page after page, with the first shaky letters of his printing and then the more confident lists as he grew used to the symbols. He would sit at the kitchen table, the radio humming behind from the mantelshelf as he worked after tea. 'Half an hour I'll give it, love. Just that much, then I'm going to watch the telly.'

'Fair enough,' she said. 'Fair enough. You're excused from the dishes.'

She was hugging to herself the triumph of a few days back when Ted had roared into the house frustrated by one of the pumps at the dam. 'Where's that bloody spanner, love, the small one?'

She looked at him for a moment, smiled and pulled a

writing pad over. On it she printed: *It is on the bloody top shelf near the sugar.* And handed the pad across and waited.

Ted picked up the pad, glared, made reading movements with his lips and burst out laughing.

'So that's how you spell it! There's other words you can be writing down for me,' he said. 'Not that I'd use them in front of a lady.'

He went over to the shelves, grabbed the spanner, gave a thumbs-up sign and headed out to the paddock.

Things picked up speed after that. He got through the final preparatory readers in another week and Janet found him one morning working his way painfully down the front page of the local weekly. 'Don't keep me out of the scandal,' she said. 'What's the council up to now?'

He stumbled through a paragraph or two, then threw the paper down in disgust with himself. 'Too hard. Too bloody hard.'

'That was fine,' she said. 'Just fine, Ted. You don't need my beady eye on you while you do it. Take it up the dunny. If it gets too much you can always wipe your bum on it.'

It became a matter of pride with him. It was pride and an evaluation of his own self that kept him persisting through another month, that kept him printing out words over and over after tea in the evenings. He became faster at the whole business and one day Janet brought him back from Red Plains' library a copy of *On Our Selection* and a selected Lawson. 'Try them,' she suggested. 'Take your time. Just bits here and there if you feel like it.'

'There's one I really liked,' he said a week later. 'About geraniums. "Water Them Geraniums." I liked that. And I've managed another. "Hungerford." Sounds like here.'

Right through winter.

With the first official day of spring, Ted was managing most of the *Red Plains Gazette* as well. She had used all kinds of pretexts to get him to read to her. She couldn't find her glasses. She'd left them in the car somewhere. Her head was aching. She had to get dinner. Could he read her out that bit about the new sewerage scheme – she'd seen the headlines. He fell for these ploys at first, but after he became aware he still good-naturedly plodded on, stumbling, hesitant, yet all the time becoming faster and more assured. She borrowed short westerns and detective stories from the library and was repaid by the joy she felt when she was the first to switch off her reading lamp while Ted, glasses perched on the end of his nose, kept negotiating with gun-slingers in Nevada.

'I love you, Ted,' she told him. 'I'm proud of you, you literate old booger!'

'I'm proud of me,' Ted had said, grinning.

She blinked and blinked at intruding memories that threatened to topple her from her stool behind the counter.

STRANGER IN TOWN

Do you remember an inn, Miranda?

Except that wasn't her name and she felt she had been living on planes and trains non-stop for a year. Howls of frustration for that past week when no one had met her at the airport at the Curry – well, it was six-thirty a.m. – and a kindly sheep farmer who was picking up stores from the light plane on the milk-run, as the locals called it, had offered her a lift into town and dropped her at the ghastly motel with its killer-green walls, dripping shower and greasy bedspread.

Still no one showed and the clock ticked by into mid-morning, the hours broken by a walk through the deserted main street and a lemon squash at one of the two pubs where a row of gummy old men stared resentfully when she breasted the bar, as if they thought she were some superannuated hooker from the coast. And still no one showed, so finally, rankling, she had rung the high-school headmaster who was supposed to be organising the whole thing and he'd said, 'I'm busy now.' Not even 'Drop up to the house and have a cup of tea with the wife.' So then she had asked the motel manager when the next plane out left and was told not until tomorrow, lady, but there's a bus.

Caught it.

Missed a gig.

Anyway, anyhow, simply a one-day yap to bored housewives interested in discussion groups – be your own poet laureate in twenty minutes, take a novel apart and rewrite it in forty. I mean! She'd have some explaining to do to the department in Brisbane who'd sent her on the strength of two slim vols – critical essays and travel pieces – to take this culture kick to the underprivileged outback. She thought this and then hated herself for lack of sympathy, for her own barbarous attitude, for . . . well, excuse me, but that last place! Surely someone could have met her even if it was so early. No taxis in a town that size and the leader of the women's group was the wife of that surly-voiced headmaster – but no, he taught mathematics. Say no more!

By the time the bus had rolled into Townsville there was a baggage handlers' strike at the airport, and here she was again riding the night train down to Rockhampton, her bag slung onto the rack above, sitting up, for the railways weren't interested in sleepers for halfway passengers, only tourists going all the way. Yes, here she was sticking to the programme and filling in for an absent writing-group tutor and heading for a two-cow town unreachable except by another train or another bus.

From the buffet car she bought a cup of tea and a bun and wobbled back between carriages, slops spattering her clothes and the bun skidding off the plate to a murky corner of her seat. How can I stand all this joy? she wondered.

But, 'Allow me,' a voice had said while she was smearing at stains, and there he was, an autumnal fellow with flattened grey hair – God! he could give her thirty years if he could give her a week – a Glaswegian accent and the suggestion of a nervous twitch to one side of his mouth.

Evie watched him as he scrabbled for the bun and held the tea for her until she'd become seated, watched him return to his seat across the aisle, unpack an apple and polish it with a crisp hanky and then cut it with a fruit knife into triangular bite-sized pieces. She tried not to look, especially after he proffered her a piece on the end of his knife, but there were only the two of them in this part of the carriage, the landscape was blotted by night and there was nowhere else to look. 'Care for some?' he had asked. 'No,' she said, forcing a smile. 'No thank you.' And he had gone on munching and glancing quickly when anyone passed through the carriage, looking back quickly at her, at his own reflection in the darkened glass of the window, and beyond his own reflection to hers.

But the ice had been broken and it was only natural, wasn't it, that remarks, mere patches of words, desultory of course, should pass between them.

She read. She dozed. She would look up and find his eyes on her, eyes that were quickly shuttered and turned away. But he was never quick enough. She had been thumbing through a collection of Lawrence's essays and she thought angrily, unfairly, she had never read greater crap. As on Hardy and the dual Will. His capitals! she thought sourly. Those pansy capitals! Their shallow typographical self-importance. 'The dual Will we call the Will-to-Motion and the Will-to-Inertia . . . And the Will-to-Motion we call the male will or spirit and the Will-to-Inertia the female.'

'Crap!' she said aloud, almost rousing the elderly Scot across the aisle from his dozing. She wouldn't concede Lawrence's next philosophic assertion: 'This will to inertia is not negative and the other positive.' She looked up and across at her not quite sleeping fellow passenger and decided that women, remembering all the women she had known, excepting those privileged rich bitches and embracing those who might have been colliers' wives in Eastwood, had solved man's problem of seeking the source of eternal motion. On the go on the go on the go. The housewife drudging eternally. She wanted to lean across and shake that natty leg into full wakefulness and demand to know who had packed his bag, who had polished that apple, remembered to include the fruit knife. She couldn't repress what galloped from her mouth. 'Ah garbage!' she said, staring down at her selection from *Phoenix*. 'Total garbage.'

'Good book?' he asked. He was that sort of man.

'Yes,' she said. 'It's a literary thriller. You know how they are.'

'I didn't think,' he said, 'that Lawrence wrote literary thrillers.'

Uh-oh! Boobed! And in any case she knew, in the fair area of her heart, that she wasn't altogether right about D. H. L., who had his moments of gender generosity – uterus envy almost, to parody that old penis king, Sigmund F.

She bit her lip with surprise and stared past him at the shuddering dark and agreed, well, yes, of course he was right. She was simply cross from having lived out of bags for a week in godawful towns where no one turned up, or if they did they had only the most primitive notions of what she was there for. It was like stepping into a sluggish mire of clones, she explained. Once in the States it had happened, somewhere in Texas, a town full of stetsons, high-heeled cowboy boots and spurs. Even the women. She couldn't help grinning at the memory, but not at this trim oddball who had perked up at the word 'Texas'. She explained her employment, the makeshift nature of her cultural forays into the wilderness, and he said that he was rather like that, the last of a dying breed, a rep, a salesman, a drummer (a Willy Loman, he offered with a sly smile), selling oriental napery, et cetera, still using the personal (hear *pairrsonal* with a fine Scottish skirling of consonants) approach, and no, he wouldn't have been on the train either except for the misfortune of a breakdown, his car suddenly demanding a gear box replacement. The whole business would take a couple of days, so . . .

'So,' she said, 'you're improving the shining hour. You couldn't face being trapped for a whole weekend in Townsville.'

He munched at a biscuit he had unwrapped from precisely folded greaseproof. 'I'd done what I could there. Thought I might as well not waste time and follow up some suggestions for sales in Rockhampton.' His mouth twitched and he turned the twitch into a smile. 'The plane strike will be over by Sunday or Monday at the latest and I'll just fly back and pick up the car.'

Yes, she had said. Yes. And there was one of those silences that expanded round the cracking of biscuit like a rotten emptiness and she returned to *Phoenix* ready to agree with Lawrence on almost everything now and somehow, uncomfortably, finding those bright eyes on her again as she read 'men only know one another in menace'.

After a while she dozed again, and was half conscious in the half-sleep before oblivion that *Phoenix* had dropped to the floor. Drowsily she sensed the pressure of another body in the seat beside her, knew somehow that her book had been picked up and replaced in her lap, and knew, too, the stroking measures of a hand on her thigh. In her slumber she brushed the hand away, mumbling something, a protest, a dismissal, but the hand returned persistent about her knee. Yet when the train pulled in to Mackay with a grinding of brakes and door slammings, she snapped awake to find her book on the seat beside her, the salesman looking at her across a chaste diagonal space and asking, 'Like another cup of tea? I'll fetch it.'

She inspected those sharp blue eyes, the gentlemanly grey of his hair, the nervous tic, the thin white skin stretched over fastidious bones. She found him unforgivable.

'No,' she said, 'thank you,' wanting to shout at him, name him a creep, a sleaze, but turning instead to watch the stragglers on the platform heading to the exit, the glare of light under the high iron roof, the ticket collector half asleep as he waved the departing passengers through.

'Well, I think I will,' he said.

After he had gone she went to the lavatory, then brushed her untidy hair, staring unforgivingly at her not quite ordinary features that had hardened years ago into a permanent creation of her late twenties and would evolve no further, apart from the scrawled comments of sun, until she was at least fifty. She hoped. She'd see to that. It was the mind, Evie had decided, that must keep its permanent interest in being, with an unflagging curiosity about the world and a capacity to maintain the inquiring wide-eyed wonder of a child. Of course, she thought, brushing angrily at obdurate knots, how does one expunge the cynicism that the simple fact of living imposes?

It was time, she decided, to grab her bag and shift to another compartment, but when she got back to her seat there was her fellow traveller holding at a half-tilt two slopping beakers of tea that dripped down his wrists and onto a paper bag of sandwiches.

'There.' He placed the lot on the pull-out table and began a fastidious mopping at hands and shirt front. 'Would you care to join me?'

Too late! Ungraciously, sulkily, she accepted the proffered tea. And then he said, 'What else do you read? Do you like Borges? Eco? Grass?'

Jee-sus! she thought, stirring her tea with a wooden spatula, what do we have here? A rep with culture?

'I get a lot of time,' he said, enjoying her blinking reaction, 'in the evenings.' Pause. 'In these desperate towns.' He smiled as if in apology. 'I wasn't always in napery. I used to travel for a publishing company years ago.'

'Quite a change of direction,' she said, 'book jackets to table napkins.'

'It gets me away.' The tic began working furiously at the corner of his mouth. 'I get up to Manila, Hong Kong. The trips do me good.' He smiled again. 'When I'm home there isn't much time for reading. My wife isn't . . . well, she's not into books and the little girls are fierce swimmers. Sport. It's kind of a religion, isn't it?'

And then he had (why? why?) hauled out a wallet and displayed family photos, dragged down his suitcase and exhibited neatly packed (emblematic patterns, she guessed, of orthodoxy) exotic Eastern wares. She made all the right noises and inwardly longed to muss the prissy rectangular precision. Her own bag was a small hold-all with a change of underwear, two skirts and a couple of tops rammed in beside textbooks and teaching notes. Should she display it for the perfect turn-off? Because by now they had exchanged names and he was beginning to press once more too eagerly forward. The twinsetted wife in the family photo would hardly approve, though Evie doubted whether the small girls with their chlorine-reddened eyes would care.

She submitted to conversation. It could erode the hours.

He'd been a lay preacher, he admitted, in his church in Brisbane, and perhaps, he surmised, that had been the starting point for his interest in reading. She doubted that but did not say, urging the train to greater speeds through the heavy dark. He had begun patting her knee to emphasise the points he made.

'Well, fancy,' he said, tapping each word in as if to underscore his statement, 'meeting a young woman who reads a good book. I do like that!'

She resented both hand and assumption and shifted back in her seat. 'There's a lot of us. A lot. In fact, lending library figures show that women are their best customers –'

'Yes. But what are they reading?'

'And further,' ignoring him and the smile that had become fixed under his blue stare, 'they are not hunched over tinnies gawping at sport on the box. Now, are they?' And she treated him to what she thought was an enchanting smile with an acidulous edge.

Enchanted only, he gave a nod. 'Point taken, my dear.' (My dear!) 'Now, my wife,' – he didn't really want to talk about his wife but the words sprang almost irrepressibly from his tongue – 'reads light romances when she does read. I wouldn't call that a nourishing diet.'

'Perhaps she's missing something in her own life,' Evie couldn't resist saying but he had a capacity to hear only what he wanted to hear. 'And anyway it's better than no diet at all. Do you realise that nearly one-third of the population cannot read or are ineffectual readers – and most of them are chaps?'

She leaned back and looked at her watch.

Half an hour to go. Thirty interminable minutes.

Abruptly she stood up and took her bag down from the rack. He was watching her sharply. She could feel his eyes follow every movement she made.

'I'm getting off too.'

'Are you?' She heard the indifference of her voice. 'Well, I'm catching the rail-motor from Rockhampton, so we probably won't see each other again.'

Outside the train the countryside was emerging in the pre-dawn light, misty hills and cane fields blurred silver under an uncertain sun blundering its way through clouds. She was back in her corner watching houses and roads take shape through the glass when once more she felt pressure on the seat beside her.

'Look,' he was saying. 'Look. Just a minute.'

'Yes?' The curtness in her voice failed to cut him off.

'Forgive a wee insanity,' he said pleadingly, leaning forward, 'but . . .' He hesitated and held her eye. 'Would you marry me if I weren't married already? Would you?'

Was he mad? What was there to say to this spontaneous idiocy?

The train was slowing down now through the outer sprawl of the town. In a moment they would be pulling in to a platform busy with welcomers and farewellers. She shook her head, unbelieving. A lay preacher! The modifier made her laugh suddenly in his face and then regret the sound that seemed to swipe him across his opened eager mouth.

Although there was hard sunlight eye-blindingly bright in the dry air, there was a darkness about the town, an ingrown self-sufficiency of secrets. She had been sensible of these emotions before, even alone in bushland – especially there – of being an intruder. A world of gum trees, bark stripping, dangling, their bony limbs rejecting grace, crowded arrogant as beggars in their rags. Once, she recalled, she had been walking alone outside a town like this, filling an hour beyond lunch, when suddenly she found herself wildly running, running, gasping and panting in unidentifiable terror, from the small glade that had delighted her eye and lurching, stumbling through regiments of indifferent trees until she ended up, heaving and winded, near the outlying houses.

At Drylands two middle-aged women had been waiting to take charge of her, whisking her by car to the town's one hotel. There were introductions – Win Briceland, Paddy Locke. The Lizard's sign dangled loose from an upstairs verandah. 'Leave your bag. It's quite safe. Someone will take it up. There's only four of us,' Win apologised. 'Well, a town this size. Unfortunately it's the line-dancing week in Red Plains. Otherwise . . .' Her voice tailed off. The other, older, woman smiled.

In the school of arts, an architectural survival of the twenties, tables and chairs had been set up by an open side door through which there was an outer view of pepper trees acting as a skirt for the Rock that shoved its ominous finger into the unclouded blue. Evie swallowed disappointment at the lack of takers. Or was it relief? She nodded and smiled at the two younger women sitting almost like schoolkids at the tables.

'As you can see,' Win said, 'there are only a few of us eager for culture.' She uttered the last word self-mockingly and won smiles from the rest. She was a busty woman with the assurance that comes from living in a small town, of knowing and being known. 'Lannie. Ro.'

Evie sat down with them. All watched with expectant eyes and waited. Why had they come? What did they expect? She was beginning to understand the isolation of these places that drove people to seize any opportunity for escape from humdrummery. These four – these pleasant four – were playing truant from husbands who regarded their activity as female folly. They were fighting the darkness.

The start of it.

Evie spoke for a few minutes, outlining the programme

for the next day. She watched their eager faces, noted the worn hands, the care with which they had dressed for this, and her sympathy brought on a dreadful urge to cry. They were here to help each other, she told them. Destructive comments were out. *Con*structive was what was wanted. She hit the first syllable and smiled. They all smiled back.

Tentatively she asked about background. Win wrote up reports for the CWA. Paddy had been a stringer for a north-coast paper. Lannie and Ro simply wagged their heads. Evie understood. She thought she understood. 'First,' she said, apologetic eyelids the teeniest flutter down, fringed fingers shaking the possibility of unpleasantness away, 'don't expect too much from me. No miracles.' They laughed dutifully. 'I can't make you creative. But I know you know that. No one can do that except God. But that's another matter. You see,' and her eyes pleaded with them to see, 'you could learn everything possible about musical composition, say, harmony, counterpoint. You could know all your chords, intervals, time patterns, the lot, and yes, you could probably, perhaps probably, put together a sonata or a symphony simply by following the rules. But would it be Mozart or Beethoven? Nothing could give you their gift of invention or melody. That's the divine gift. And I might add, I don't have it either.' A self-deprecating grin. 'We'll work at it together. Are you with me?'

They all said they were with her. She was hating her-self. These weary expectant faces!

'And so all I can suggest or all we can suggest together,' (bugger prolixity, she thought, and packed a radiance like any pistol-packin tutor) 'are ideas about structure, character development, variations in sentence form, ways to sharpen dialogue without a plethora of he saids, she saids. That sort of thing. Little tricks. Are you with me?'

They were still with her. And she saw their eyes light up with possibility because this day was different with the pleasure of simply cutting loose from the ordinariness of the other-day grind in even this simplest of ways. And while someone made tea and others produced scones and cake, she hated herself and what she was supposed to be doing, floundering between their hope and their hopelessness.

The Lizard was roaring when she returned late that afternoon, the bar racketing with the desperate grogships formed after the third glass, sustained by a matiness of tired old catchwords but waiting for the peril of the imagined insult, the disagreements after the sixth or seventh.

She walked along the one street and found a café still open where she picked at a chop and salad under the flicker-eye of the waitress. She kept thinking of a woman she had met in the last coastal town a week back, a handsome, wry-mouthed blonde who was teaching in the boondocks and had come in for a weekend break. She was filling in time, she confessed, enduring the teaching and on the threshold of marrying.

'That's some threshold,' Evie had said. 'That's certainly some threshold. Is he a teacher too?'

The blonde had been enormously amused. 'He's an itinerant pineapple picker.'

'But do you, well, have much in common?' Evie couldn't hold back the question.

'Just about everything.'

That was a stopper!

Later she thought it might have been more a comment on teaching.

They'd met again at the home of a local who was giving a polite farewell party for Evie. The blonde was an expert – is *diseuse* the word? – who had plumped herself down at the living-room piano mid-drinks and begun reciting as she played heart-rending old folklore, bush ballads – whatever – with a polish and style that belonged to an alien time, say sixty years ago. Her voice was husky with emotion mimed for laughs.

Would her skewed talent survive the pineapples? Evie couldn't gauge the parameters of desperation.

She walked back to the pub and started up the stairs to her room. A figure blocked the ill-lit landing and there he was again, the traveller from the night train, watching her ascent, his whole body eager for recognition. There came a babble of words: he'd hired a car on the coast, done some business in Red Plains, he had to see her, he was off the next day, he couldn't get her out of his mind, he . . .

Perhaps his persistence was for laughs too.

He appeared to be blocking her doorway.

She shoved past him.

'Not my threshold!' she said, irrelevantly for him and not caring if she hurt, and closed the door.

Next morning the class began its readings.

Win, Paddy, Lannie, Ro.

She had set the simplest of assignments, unsure what their regular tutor suggested. Working blind.

With the exception of Paddy Locke, the oldest group member, who described her willing exile in Drylands with a kind of amused zest, they read small pieces so polite, so tentative they became mounds of indistinguishable dullness – bushfires, floods, trips to the coast. Yet every now and again there would be a light, dry moment that hinted at a cynicism, a humour, an eye for the odd. A sentence here, a sentence there that Evie felt – no, knew – pointed to a sensitivity that was being repressed in case it transgressed the boundaries of what the writer was supposed to feel, that broke through those sanctions imposed by the conventions of thinking acceptable for small-town bush wives.

One hour. Two. At tea-break she said, unable to hold

back any longer, 'Don't any of you hate anyone? Love anyone? Aren't there any scandals, adulteries, generosities, shy kindnesses or petty meannesses, reprobates, criminals, heroes even? Anything? Anything that creates conflict, brings tears? Isn't this town ...' pause ... 'a normal hotbed of jealousies, loyalties, goodwill?'

Shocked, they stared at her, then two or three of the women began to laugh.

'Nothing we could talk about.'

'Or write about.'

'There'd be a reckoning.'

'What sort of reckoning?'

'Violence,' Lannie whispered.

She looked at them: Win, Paddy, Lannie, Ro.

There was a silence that stretched a glassy film across the old hall with its dusty stage, its uncleaned windows, its notices of the dance before the dance before last, the screamer poster of a rock band that failed to show with a 'cancelled' strip pasted across, a noticeboard with typed memos of CWA meetings.

'They don't like it,' Lannie said. 'Our coming to classes. My old man didn't want me to come. Thought it might give me ideas. He seems to think we're trying to be something we haven't any right to be.'

'Maybe. Maybe.' Evie smiled through a mouthful of scone. 'Perhaps he's frightened you'll write about him. Frightened he'll feature in a blockbuster!'

'Blockbuster's the word,' someone whispered and they all laughed then and the bonds strengthened. It was like feeling muscle grow, expand, attach to other muscle and fuse without tissue rejection. 'Do it, love,' a voice urged. 'There's a lot of us could do it.' And Evie was aware as she had not been aware of certain giveaway lines about mouths and eyes, a tightening of lips despite that country-woman calm that spoke of baked dinners and hefty breakfasts and, between the dinners and breakfasts and the morning and afternoon scones and pikelets, hours spent on tractors or hay-balers or early evening milkings, interspersed with washing and ironing and carting the kids miles to the nearest school bus and fetching them back, all wedged in before a spot of mending or clothes-making and grubbing around the vegetable plot.

'And after all that,' Lannie said as if Evie had listed their husbands' demands aloud, 'we help the kids with their homework while the men go off to the pub for their quiet time.'

That broke them up. Their yelps of laughter restored lost confidence. There they all were, Win, Paddy, Lannie, Ro, calm again but tight with that underlay of resentment surfacing above the neat starched cottons, the shampooed hair, the vestige of makeup that reassured them they were not simply milkers, tractor drivers, cleaners and cooks.

'Blockbuster,' Ro repeated. 'That's the word!'

Evie looked at her with interest. Ro bore the dying thundercloud of a blackened eye. There was still swelling across one cheekbone. Her left arm was in a sling. The rest of the group saw Evie wonder and were embarrassed and knowing.

'The thing is to write about what you know, what you really know.' Evie turned her gaze deliberately away from bruised flesh. 'What you feel.'

The morning moved on towards midday. 'After lunch I'll get you to write a few hundred words or so, as I said, about what you really feel. The things that mean most to you.' And she offered to take their material with her if there wasn't time to go through it with them that afternoon. She promised to return the material with comments. 'Helpful, I hope,' she said and watched them smile at each other, still united by laughter. She handed out photocopies of stories by Chekhov, Hemingway, Carver, Updike. 'We'll look at these now. They'll show you, tell you lots of things.'

During the lunch-break one of the women manned the tea urn and the rest of them took cups and sandwiches out onto the lawn and sat in the shade of the pepper trees.

They had only begun to pass plates around when a truck pulled up on the road with an angry screech of rubber and two men got out, slammed car doors and started towards the group. 'See that man,' Win, the group leader, said softly to Evie and pointing to the plumper, shorter fellow, 'that's my husband. He is *the* cultural desert.' She smiled into her cup.

The two walked with a bushman's roll and halted, legs wide apart, a few paces from the women, threat and animosity in their stance. Win's husband briefly touched his hat brim before both hands vanished into pockets. Again Evie sensed darkness in the bright air.

Words came in chunks.

'Need the wives,' the other man said. He was tall and sinewy, his face carved sharp as an axe-blade. He looked at and through them all. 'Need a hand back at the farm.' He stared brazenly at Evie. 'Didn't know the missus was goin in for this sort of stuff. Okay, Ro, pack it in now and let's get goin.'

Ro dropped her blackened eyelids and shuffled papers and handbag together. Evie went over to her and whispered, 'You don't have to go. Remember what I said.'

Ro nodded without once looking up.

'Shake it up there!' the man ordered. 'Right now, mate. You must of forgot lunch, eh?'

His horrible joviality fell into a flattened moment. He was hurling words at his shrinking wife like clods or bricks and she was not dodging but receiving like a willing saint, enduring abuse as a terrible balm.

'God, Howie,' Win complained, 'you said you'd be

okay. I left your lunch in the fridge. Can't you open the door, eh?'

'It's not that, Win,' the other man interjected. His grin didn't reach his eyes. 'He's comin over to me and there's the hands to feed, the two boys helpin with the yarding, eh. Come on, Ro. Look snappy!'

Ro shrank back against the tree as if she might burrow into its sheltering bark. The rest of the women looked down at their untouched plates. 'Well, I'm not coming,' Win said firmly to her husband. 'I arranged this day weeks back and you knew about it.' There were bright spots of red on her cheeks. 'And I don't think Ro should have to go either.'

'Mind your own business, love,' Ro's husband said. 'I don't give a stuff what you do. That's Howie's problem. But Ro comes now. Come on, woman! Do I have to bloody drag you out?'

Evie stood up and went forward till she was close enough to smell sweat and beer and the unpleasant stink of withheld rage.

'How dare you burst in like this! The class is taking a lunch-break before the afternoon session. I need them all here this afternoon.'

The man swivelled and stared.

'And who the fuck are you? Some two-bit bitch teacher from the city out to see how the other half lives. Get out of my way!'

His mouth was soured from failure and a need to bully. He elbowed Evie to one side and trod brutishly through the little group towards his wife whose face, white and tight with humiliation, bulged with tears that she pinched back. Dragging at her arm he jerked her up roughly.

'That's assault!' Evie shouted. 'I'll get the police!'

Win's husband was backing off. 'Okay, Wal, give it a rest. We'll take the crew down to the pub.'

'Jesus! You gonna be pushed round by some fuckin woman?' Wal pulled Ro forward and gave her a hefty whack across the back. 'Get goin, love, before I have to hand you one.'

'I'm not coming,' Ro whispered.

'What? What you say?'

'I'm not coming.'

The man drew his arm back like a paddle and swung his palm forward in one savage movement that cracked the bone of her cheek. She let out a small scream and fell forward, her hands digging at the grass.

'Want some more?' he asked. 'Or you got the message yet? You always was slow to get the message.' His boot nudged her shoulder as she lay, nudged, drew back and drove in harder.

'For God's sake!' Win cried and her voice broke into her husband's inertia so that, shamed, he ran forward and wrestled Wal away. The two men struggled for a moment, and then as suddenly as the tussle had begun it ended with Wal stalking off towards the truck. 'Okay,' he shouted back over his shoulder. 'Okay. But you know what'll be waiting for you later. God, I can't wait!'

The truck roared off in explosions of bulldust but the whole weather of the day had darkened. No one knew what to say. Nothing could muffle the little gasps and whimpers of Ro who had been so demeaned.

Someone had fetched ice from the esky and was holding it to Ro's cheek. Another was helping her sip hot tea. 'It's all right,' Win kept assuring. 'It's all right, love. We all knew.'

Evie couldn't repress the words that fell out of her mouth almost unwilled. 'Well, I hate to say it but that was something – something to write about.'

The group looked at her, shocked.

She couldn't explain what had made her say that. She was shaking. 'It's a help,' Evie argued. 'You'd be surprised at what a help it is.' Could she explain her own lost marriage to them, the months of disillusion with a gambler's broken promises, the poverty, the debts, the emptied bank accounts – until she finally walked out? It had hardened her. She knew that and detested it.

'We help,' Win said. 'We try to help.'

'Well,' Evie persisted with the impertinence of an outsider, a blow-in. She looked at the ruins of the day, the discarded lunch, the injured woman, the broken but loving attempts to assuage, and decided to say what she felt must be said. 'Ro can't stay with that bastard. There's a refuge on the coast. She's got to do something. He'll end up killing her.'

'It's the kids,' Ro mumbled. 'Can't leave the kids. They're still in primary.'

The group nodded as if one.

'Take them with you,' Evie said. 'Think of yourself for a change.' She could have wept for them. 'It was just an idea. I'm single now. I was married, but, well, you know how it is. I've forgotten.'

They told her she didn't understand. They told her how small the town was. They told her the police wouldn't act. The police always took the husband's side in these matters. The police drank with them. They wouldn't do anything to upset a mate.

Back at the pub she showered and changed into fresh clothes. Two hours before the rail-motor pulled out. She kept seeing Ro's battered face, kept hearing her whimpers as she was dragged up from the grass. No more, she thought. I can't come to these places any more.

She lay back on her bed and began reading through the papers she had collected from the women and would later post back with comments. Outside the sun settled in a blaze of yellow behind the Rock. From below came the steady hum of the early drinkers. She was packed. She was ready to leave. She put the papers aside and wondered whether she should head up the street for another dreary meal at the local café, with the flies drumming against the window and the moths rushing to death on the light bulbs.

There was a slight noise at her half-opened door, a cough, a token tapping, and she swung about to see him once more – she couldn't believe it! – the man from the train, the traveller in soft goods, still light, still bouncy, peering foggily from behind his glasses. He wore his assurance like a flower behind the ear.

'Ah,' he said, entering, 'there you are! I've been hanging around all day, shuffling between Red Plains and here. What a town!'

'Please leave,' she said. 'Please.'

She rose and walked across the room but he stood firm and resisted her push with a stolidity that held a wiry threat. Suddenly she was afraid.

'Why did you wait?' she asked him. He had rented a car. There was nothing to stay for. But he regarded her with his sweetly ascetic smile and tried holding her eyes meaningfully, so that she felt sorry for him at the same time, for his stupidity, for that mordant puritanism looking for a quick lay he could excuse on the grounds of irresistible attraction or love. Deprivation? It meant nothing. Later he would confess to his wife and pass on the burden. A moment! Just like that! It meant nothing, he would tell her. Nothing. And he would feel good and go outside and water the garden.

'I thought you might like a lift.'

Evie found herself thinking, in the middle of her fright, like a filmic five-second grab, Now, here's a story my little group could have fantasised about, approximately two thousand words, double-spaced, leave a two-inch margin.

'I don't think so. I'm going out to eat. Let me past.'

'I'll join you.'

'No.'

She thrust by him and ran quickly down the stairs into the desolation of the main street. A light still showed in the newsagency across the road and she caught a glimpse of a woman on the balcony above. For the briefest of moments their eyes met and she saw the woman's head move in a negating fashion. Then she was gone and Evie walked along the street to the café and pushed in through dangling fly-hazard and sat at a corner table. He darted in quickly behind her and sat opposite, watching while she pretended to read the menu.

'Go away.' She could hear herself hissing.

'I don't think so. Not yet. Not now. You mustn't make a scene, my dear.'

Behind the counter the waitress regarded them indifferently, resting her weight on one foot. She walked slowly to their table. It was the end of the day and she'd had it. She was a heartbreakingly pretty fifteen-year-old who hadn't yet thought of escape. The evening's date was sufficient to look forward to. Evie gave her order and saw the man run his eyes over the girl, inspecting swiftly, assessingly, before saying, 'Just tea.'

Evie was conscious of irrational and ferocious pique. She should leave. She should ignore him. She should remain silent. But, 'Why did you wait?'

'I had to.'

'Had to?'

'Had.' He forgot the waitress for a moment and gave her another of his infinitely sad, infinitely hypocritical smiles.

'There's never "had to",' Evie said. 'There's never compulsion. We're free as air.'

'Ah. You don't understand, do you, the force of a once-in-a-million . . . chance of it . . . of meeting. The fact that out of all . . . that train . . . the way we talked . . . the car breakdown . . . The . . . well . . . all those imponderables.'

This was dated stuff. It could have come from a late-night forties movie. Of course, she admitted to herself as she munched her salad, it was verbally more attractive than 'How about a fuck?' But less honest.

His light blue eyes, Evie realised, could not decide

96

between her and the waitress, but when she had finished her meal and gathered up her shoulder bag he insisted on walking her back to the hotel.

'No,' she said. 'Get away.'

But there he was beside her hurrying feet, beside her as she sped up the stairs to collect the rest of her luggage, and there, inside the room once more, the door slammed to, his back against it.

'We've got to talk.'

'We've done that. Get out! Get away from that door!'

He took it like a champ with punches in reserve, that smile still on his flattened face. 'Not yet,' he said, barring her way. 'I've got problems. Problems.' His voice began to rise and become shrill. 'My wife. My kids. You don't understand.'

'Oh, I bloody understand!' she shouted. 'I certainly do that. Let me past! Let me bloody past.'

He grabbed her and waltzed her over towards the bed, throwing her backwards onto the sheets. His strength shocked. She was too terrified to scream, too busy fighting his mauling hands, writhing, shoving, finally clawing one side of his face as she tumbled from the narrow bed, striking her cheek against the corner of the bedside table. She yelled out in pain, feeling blood run between her fingers, watching his face become suddenly appalled as he stood up and stepped back.

'You shit!' she screeched, mopping at her face. 'You shit shit shit!'

She was deaf to his protests, his iterated apologies. She grabbed her bags and slammed into the passageway, almost falling down the stairs and out through the front door beyond the rising cries of the drinkers. Ro's husband was standing in the bar doorway, the centre of drunken laughter, and she saw him see her as she stumbled past. He mock-toasted her with his schooner glass slopping over but she ignored the salute, the howl of amusement, and dodged round the rear of his parked truck. Blood kept trickling down her cheek while she half strode, half ran to the railway station. She scrubbed her face with her arm, smearing it, not caring. She did not once look back.

The train was in and waiting. This was indeed the end of the line.

She took a seat in the last carriage as close as she could to the guard's cubicle, glancing around quickly to see if she was alone, but across the aisle a huddled group was watching as she slung her bags onto the rack.

The swollen cheek, the bruised eye, two small kids in pyjamas half asleep. Ro looked defiantly at her for a moment, then managed a half-smile. Evie threw her hands apart in a nothing-to-declare fashion and moved her head slowly from left to right, left to right, as the woman above the newsagency had done. The train let

98

out its own dingo cry as it started up and shuddered along the track. Beyond the shaken windows the world was black on black.

Two of a kind.

She would write a story, she decided, about a woman in an upstairs room above a main street in a country town, writing a story about a woman writing a story.

MEANWHILE . . .

'Is it a boy or a drudge?' her mother had asked the matron in the cottage hospital delivery room.

'A drudge, dear,' the matron said. And winked.

The story was repeated all over town.

Mother was a goer, a bit of a dasher in that small coastal village. Her outspokenness caused raised eyebrows and pursed lips. The daughter of a mill owner in the sugar belt, she was an only child who received a boarding-school education and had gained a formidable matriculation pass at the outbreak of World War II. A maths freak. Despite her father's objections to higher education for women she went to university and graduated in science the year of the bombing of Pearl Harbor. Then she had attended teachers' college for a year and at the end of that time found herself appointed to a high school at a liberating distance from her home.

With most of the male staff enlisted or conscripted she took all the senior forms in physics, chemistry and maths for a salary sixty percent of the male rate. She didn't like that. She didn't like being charged the same amount as the bank clerks for board at the hotel where she spent her evenings marking assignments. She didn't like paying the same fare on buses to get to work. In fact, she insisted early on that she would pay only sixty percent of the fare. This caused some difficulty but the bus driver's son was in his final year at high school and hoped to matriculate into a reserved course at university, like engineering or medicine, and so avoid the draft. His bus-driver daddy allowed her to win the argument.

Mother was almost beautiful, a poised, calm young woman with symmetrical features and a rush of long black hair that she wore pulled back into a loose but entrancing knob. Its wafting insecurity offered many opportunities for her to raise her arms in a careless balletic style to pin it up. She appeared unaware of the attractiveness of this.

She had been teaching for two years when the war ended and in an unguarded moment married a returned soldier whose sheer stupidity had ensured his commission. In the swiftness of courtship she failed to notice this also. After a brief honeymoon in Sydney they returned to the coastal town where he was assistant manager at

104

another sugar mill. The woman accountant who had been filling in for him was sacked immediately and life proceeded, for him at least, as it had always done, but this time in a hot rented house not far from the mill.

Robert was a what's-for-dinner and there's-a-button-missing-on-my-shirt man. She noticed those things very quickly. Her world, at that point, tilted on its axis. Within the year she was pregnant. 'No more teaching for you,' her husband said. 'You'll have two of us to look after. That'll take all your time.' He seemed rather glad to be saying this. After all it was conservative 1947. In a town that size it was not done to have a working wife.

'What do they call this stuff, then?' she had asked, pointing to a large basket of dirty linen, waving a hand towards the oven and its half-roasted leg of lamb.

'That's different,' he said. 'That's what wives are expected to do.'

'I've been at school all day.'

'Well, now that's all going to end.' He smiled. She was beginning to hate his smile.

When Janet was four the local high school pleaded with her mother to return, at least for the matriculation class, suggesting regular part-time work five mornings a week. Mother jumped at it and there followed days, weeks of terrible argument based mainly on the premise that the house and its demands would be neglected.

'You mean *your* demands,' she heard her mother say.

Janet became very busy with colouring in. By making herself as unobtrusive as possible – there were many corners – she learned a lot about the eternal warfare of married couples. It rather put her off.

'Never mind, dear,' her mother said to her as they started out for school that first week, Janet having been taken into kindergarten class a year early as a special favour, 'things will improve.'

They didn't. But she learnt to read in that first year and learnt also to move quietly outside to her swing under the strangler fig when words began flying like gravel.

The gravel flew for a year, and then one morning her mother packed several bags and enlisted the help of the bus driver's wife whose son had not only won a scholarship to university but had completed a dazzling final year in engineering. 'I can't thank you enough,' his mother said as she dropped the runaway pair at the railway station in Rockhampton. 'Good luck, my dears, and if there's anything . . .' Et cetera, et cetera.

Father didn't bother to pursue. Within the month he simply filed for divorce on the grounds of abandonment. 'A misuse of the word,' Janet's mother said. 'You will understand later.' Janet barely glanced up from a badly thumbed copy of *The Magic Pudding*. 'Always remember,' Mother said, watching her absorbed child, 'that being unable to read is being crippled for life.' Janet sucked her thumb, nodded and turned the page.

Funny how some phrases stick, she thought now, going back fifty-odd years to that moment in the Rockhampton Mail. She moved away from the window of her living-room where she had been watching a young woman hurry past the chiackings of early drinkers at the Lizard. Life had been easier after that, she remembered. Mother had resumed teaching. What else could she do? They rented a small house in South Brisbane and formed a jolly relationship unjuggled by the difference in years. Janet was six going on forty.

These days the futility of it all made her feel six.

LETTING THE LAVE GO BY

After the fifth dry year, after that, what with his age, his sixth decade peaking at the height of summer, he decided to give it away. Letting the lave go by, except that out here it was all tumbleweed and dust.

His thousand-acre patch – he had never allowed himself to toy with the metrics of space – was worthless, unable to sustain the small holding of stock that tottered to starvation bones on lack of pasture. He was in debt to the bank for fodder, for fencing, for veterinary services; and he had had enough. Even the lease of the block down by the creek to that out-of-towner, Massig, had only held the bank at bay for a short time. The creek that bounded his paddocks ran thin as his spirit – both now a series of waterholes choked by weed.

Pulling out, he told everyone in his countable town. I'm pulling out.

He sold off everything except the home paddock where the timber house groaned in the rainless air, creaked and shrank in the vertical summers. There was a shed behind the house that he needed and a further acre or two along the creek with Massig's shack. No point in turning him off. The minimum rent kept him in groceries.

I'm pulling out, he told the lot of them down at the pub.

The weather turns round, Jim, they all warned, old-hand prognosticators. 'It turns around,' Howie Briceland agreed, but happily adding another five hundred acres, even if useless, to his empire. He was a man who believed in the sorcery of large numbers. 'You're a bit of a fool. The climate's got to take a turn.'

'I'll let you wait for that,' he'd replied. 'I'll let you enjoy it when it happens. There's something I've got to do.'

And what's that? they had all asked.

But Randler wouldn't say.

Yet how he remembered that other time, that earlier time, and how the memory plagued him. And how he lusted. That was it. Lusted.

He was ten, a scraggy bit of a kid and the war over. Old philanthropies fell back into place and the far west scheme for underprivileged children who'd never been to the coast had plucked him up with half a dozen others for a week's holiday by the sea, straight through on the Western Mail and then a rackety road coach to a house on a beach outside Rockhampton where, for the first time in his ten years, his eyes were shocked by that moving world of aquamarine whose surface shook in repeated patterns of yeasty invitation.

The vastness frightened him at first. The immensity. It wasn't like the pictures he'd seen. No painting, no photograph could lift itself from a final flatness. This monster crawled. It threatened. It munched the sand stretch where he stood. 'What is it?' he'd asked the man and woman who ran the place. 'What's out there?'

'That's the sea, love,' the plump, good-natured woman said. Neither she nor her husband laughed. He was glad of that, he remembered. And then she'd ruffled his hair. 'It's real beautiful, isn't it. Look.'

None of the other kids seemed to want to know – or maybe they did know. They'd headed straight off across the sand and were splashing about at the edge of that swinging blue floor, shrieking as their pants and shirts got wet and racing back out to stand shy and scared before all this fluid power.

'What's past that, mister?' he'd asked the man.

'Past what?'

'Past all that water?'

The man had smiled then and his hands moved to touch briefly Jim's thin tense shoulders. 'If you swam straight across you'd reach America. South America. You heard of that?'

'Yes,' he said. He'd seen it on a globe at school.

'But it'd be a long swim!' The man laughed. 'You'd need a boat.'

Young Jim was a loner, not quite a misfit, but one who preferred his own company to the pack of eight-year-olds who had made the trip with him. They were from places even farther out than his own town and he didn't know any of them. He felt almost grandfatherly looking at them digging and kicking in the sand.

Then, 'Lunch, boys,' the motherly woman had said, clucky, smiling wider. And they trooped up to the house and he'd never seen so much food, all set out on a long table on the verandah, great piles of sandwiches and cakes and fruit on each plate, and the man said, mock fierce, 'Tuck in, you kids. Gotta clean the lot up now, or you'll hurt me wife's feelings, eh!' And they had giggled and tucked in, and he could still remember the happiness he'd felt, the relaxation of it all, though he didn't know the word then; and afterwards, the bunk beds made up for them in the three spare rooms and pegs to hang their clothes and everything. God, everything, he remembered. And never a scowl, a yell, a cry of anger or displeasure.

The next day, the big man, Mr Watters, seeing him mooning along the beach on his own while the smaller kids watched by his wife splashed about in the water, asked him if he'd like to go for a row in the small inlet that licked in to the beach from the south, a green creek-fed tongue of backwater separated from the sea at low tide by a sandbar. A small jetty ran out and three or four hire-dinghies were beached.

'I can't row,' he said. He'd read that word.

'Never mind,' the man said. 'It won't take you long at all.' He pulled a funny face. 'You've got the best teacher on the coast right here.'

Mr Watters went up to the boatshed and fetched oars and rowlocks then strolled over to one of the dinghies, hauled the killick from its mooring behind a lump of coral and tossed it and its rope into the belly of the boat. 'Give us a hand, mate,' he said to Jim, and began dragging the boat down to the water. Mate, the boy thought, pleased, and raced to help and then watched as the boat began to bounce and bob in the shallows.

'It's a dancer!' he cried, delighted.

'Sure is,' the man said. 'Hop in. She'll take us for a waltz, eh. Now, you just watch what I do.'

Jim perched up in the stern and watched the big man brace his feet against the thwart while he slipped the rowlocks into place and slid the oars into position. 'See. Like so. You got to watch them, mate. Mustn't lose your rowlocks.' He shoved one oar into the sand and pushed the boat out. 'Now, here's the crazy bit, eh, I row with me back to the way we're going.' And he grinned and Jim, tense with watching, with learning, laughed; and the day was hot and blue and the air smelt of salt and he'd never known anything like this, this nimble butting over water with the shore slipping behind and the gulls crying and the smaller kids who'd come up from the beach to watch waving as they slid back and back and away.

'Watch how I dip 'em,' the man said. 'Back, dip the edge of the blades, pull against the water as you lean back, then raise 'em, turning your hands so that when you reach the end of your swing they go down again clean and straight.'

They were in the centre of the lagoon now and Jim was beside himself with delight, with movement, with the lapping slap, with a brilliance of transparency. Over the side of the dinghy he could see through clear water the ribbed sand below and a moving cloud of tiny delicate fish. He wanted to ask a hundred questions but the big man said, shipping his oars, 'We're going to change places, mate. Fancy a young codger like you, eh, letting an old buffer like me row! Steady, now, gently does it or you'll tip us over.'

The dinghy wobbled crazily as Mr Watters shifted back to the stern. Jim was too excited to be nervous. He edged into place and took hold of the oars as he'd seen the man do. He was hungry to learn.

'Okay,' the man said. 'Now. Dip, pull, and swing.'

The boy was over-eager. The blades flattened.

'Never mind,' the man said, grinning. 'That's what we call catching crabs. Keep them edges sharp.'

He swung again, the oars heavy in his skinny arms, but they went down sharp and he pulled against the water and the boat shot forward.

'We're moving!' he shouted. 'We're moving!'

'You're doing great,' the big man said.

Delight knocked him silly. He pulled again and again, the knack of it becoming easier each time, and glancing over his shoulder he saw the far side of the inlet coming in at them.

'Time for port and starboard,' Mr Watters said. 'You'll be a regular old salt by the end of the day. Now, listen carefully while I tell you how to put the boat about.'

He learned how to hold one oar, how to pull it against the other. He learned fast.

'Not bad, not bad at all. You keep this up and I'll be offering you a job.'

They went backwards and forwards across the little inlet half a dozen times. He wanted never to stop but then Mr Watters said, 'That's enough for this morning, eh. You've come along fine.'

'I want to keep going,' the boy said. 'I love it.'

'I know, son. I know. But your shoulders are going to be that sore you won't thank me. We'll rub in some oil when we get back. Anyhow, I'd best get back to the others, eh, and give the missus a break.'

'Can I come out on my own then?'

'Can you swim?'

'A bit. Learnt in the creek at home.'

'Well, then. We'll see. This'll be easier. Maybe tomorrow.'

'I can't wait,' the boy said. 'I really can't wait.'

'Think you might have to,' the big man said. But he said it kindly with a grin.

The next morning Mr and Mrs Watters brought the tiddlers down to the lagoon where, buoyed by salt water and zest, they spent an hour learning to float and dog-paddle, stroking up and down in a clumsy crawl. Jim came out first and dug his bony toes through sand, kicking it in little spurts. There was a scab hanging off his knee above raw pink skin. He picked at it absent-mindedly, his mind on boats, watching the big man walking up the beach towards him.

'Can I now?' he asked. 'Please, mister? I did two widths, across and back.'

'I didn't see you,' Mr Watters said.

'You did! You did! I waved from the other side.'

'Was that you, eh? So you did. I thought it was some champ from up the coast.' The big man's eyes were very blue in the morning light and crinkled with amusement. 'Look, son, it's these young nippers keep me busy. All right, then, while we're here, scoot up the shed and get the gear.'

Jim was to remember for years the envy on the faces

of the smaller boys as they watched him drag the dinghy down to the water, put the oars in position, shove off with one foot and pull out into the lagoon.

'That's the way!' the man yelled. 'That's it!' He was being pestered and grabbed at by capering kids shrilling and yelling for a go. 'Now you've done it! Now you've started something!' But he was laughing. 'Have to run joyrides now!'

But Jim didn't hear. He was pulling away across the water in permanent summer bound for Tonga, Samoa, Tahiti: the coral islands he'd read about. 'I can row,' he heard himself say out loud. 'I can row I can row I can row.'

I can row, he told himself all the way back in the train. He told his dad, too, who looked pleased for the moment but chewed up his son's pleasure with, 'Not much call for that out here, lad,' as he looked skywards into a cobalt desert. 'But your mum would have been pleased.' He sighed. 'She was a coastal girl, all full of waves and beaches.'

Jim couldn't really remember his mother. She'd died when he was three and his father, stubbornly refusing to give his kid up to grandparents, to remarry, to do any of the things other men would have done to save themselves effort, had struggled on his own to raise his son, grappled with farm and bad weather and just scraped a living for the two of them. He managed. 'You're a bloody wonder, Davo,' his mates said. 'Couldn't do it meself. How the hell do you cope?'

But his father's comments didn't stop the boy. He planned a raft for the creek swimming-hole, a packing-case floater that could drift in the few feet of water left. The waterhole was on their property, a dank sombre place where the creek was dammed up by rock and fallen log. He imagined lying on his raft, drifting, staring at a sky checkered by the limbs of the red gums and the coolabahs. He wanted to do this on his own.

'Need any help?' his father had asked as Jim headed to the shed. The old man couldn't stop himself: 'Don't forget Archimedes' law.'

'I don't need a hand,' the boy told him, stubbornly knocking out planks from a case.

'Well, when you've done that,' his father said, hurt by rejection and a failed joke, 'I'll need a hand on the truck later with the feed runs.'

Although Jim did not want overseeing, he realised that he could never manhandle the finished raft all the way down to the creek, so he dragged the pieces there plank by plank and tried to assemble them on the sandy slope. After an hour he achieved a clumsy inexpert flat-ness of pineboards hammered onto green tea-tree branches and lashed with rope.

The moment the last lashing was tied he hauled the raft down the bank and eased it into the creek where it teetered drunkenly, with water oozing between the cracks and slopping over the surface.

Floating. But only just.

He watched with a smile, then waded in and holding it by one corner edged himself aboard until he was sitting square in the middle. Instantly it sank three inches and his pants were soaked. Furious, he paddled back to the bank and stared at his work. With his weight lifted, the raft rose once more and flopped impertinently. 'Bugger!' he shouted. 'Bugger! Bugger!' He wondered if packing the cracks with some of his dad's plastic grouter would help. He wanted to yell and howl with frustration and he screeched out all the rude words he knew.

Nothing helped.

He waded in again, shoved the raft, now much heavier with its waterlogged pine, back to the side of the creek and, gasping and tugging, managed finally to hoist it over the lip and along the bank to hide it under scrub.

When his breath came back he ran home against grass, against hot air, against himself, to be stopped mid-stride by his father who held him tight for a moment, inspecting the excitement and disappointment on the boy's crumpled face.

'So how did it go?'

'What?'

'The raft? Does it work?'

Jim was scowling through snotty tears.

'Well, does it?'

'No.'

'Then you'd better let me have a look.'

That was then. Randler could still remember that day in every detail. His dad had lugged the pineboard mess back on the tractor, puttied the cracks, added a frame and had taken it down to the creek the next morning. 'Now we'll see,' he said. 'Should be right now. I'll trim off a pole for you and you can use the raft like a punt. How about that, eh?' He paused, thinking for a moment. 'You know, it'd be better up in the house dam. Not much water there at the moment, and a lot safer. And you wouldn't have those little creeps from town coming to muck it up.'

'I want them to see it.'

He was proud of what his dad had done. He'd painted a name on it – *Kon-Tiki* – which he'd read about in a book from the town library.

'The dam would be better.'

Jim was obstinate. 'No,' he insisted. 'No. I want the creek.'

'Okay then,' his old man said. So they'd had an official launch, his dad snapping open a beer for himself and a Coke for the kid and splashing the wooden planks. 'Let's see you go.'

Afloat.

He shoved off with the pole his dad had fixed and worked his way across the waterhole to the tree barrier and back. When he lay down he could paddle with his hands, pushing over the water under the dusty gauze of leaves.

'Well, that's pretty good,' his father said. 'Pretty damn good.'

'You want a go?' the boy asked.

'No, son, no. I'd be too heavy. You'd see her sink again. Archimedes' law!'

'What's that?'

'I'll explain sometime. You go ahead, sailor.' He sat there sipping his beer slowly and watching the sun freckle the water beneath the scrub. He'd never seen his son's eyes so alight, so bright with possibilities.

'You go now, Dad,' Jim called after a while. 'I'll be okay.'

'Lunchtime,' his father said. 'I'll help you stow her. I've got to get into town afterwards. And you've got school again tomorrow. We'll have to get your duds sorted.' He wanted to take the raft home on the trailer but Jim begged for it to be left higher up the bank under the gidgee.

'So I can get at it. It'll be okay,' he argued. 'It's on our place.'

He was wrong. He couldn't stop himself from talking

123

about it at school. Howie Briceland and his gang listened, watching with small eyes. On the last day of that week when he went down to the creek he found the raft smashed to bits. Someone had taken to it with a sledge-hammer, leaving splintered pine all along the bank. Pieces had been tossed into branches on the far side and dangled like a bad joke.

'Well,' his father said, hugging the sobbing kid, 'well, son, it's a rotten trick but it's a lesson for life. Envy's a terrible thing.'

'Can you make me another?' the boy asked between snuffles. 'Can you?'

'Maybe. But you'll have to keep it up on the dam then. Listen,' he added, 'don't let them know at school, eh. Don't say a word about it being smashed up. That'll only please the little bastards.'

When the kids made snide references the next Monday, when they asked him how the raft was going, he lied and said his dad was buying him a boat on the coast and they'd keep it there.

They didn't believe him. And his dad never got round to making a second raft. And work on the farm went on endlessly with the ploughing of the near paddock for lucerne and the hay baling and the dagging and help with the dipping and the culling of sick lambs who staggered blindly dying on their feet because their mothers couldn't feed them in the drought and trucking feed out to the grazed-bare paddocks for the older ones still standing and helping with the meals after he got in from the school bus with his dad dropping dead-tired in a rocker on the verandah, eyes red and hopeless with dust.

Jim was eleven, twelve, thirteen.

He felt older than his old man.

'It's all yours,' his father would say, waving expansive arms, 'the whole godawful place. You'd better learn to make a go of it, son, because there isn't anything else.'

'Why don't we sell up?' he'd asked.

'Who'd buy it?' his father replied. 'Anyway, it's a love-hate thing, I suppose. You'll understand one of these days. It's got memories. Your mum. You. And fundamentally, son, it's all we've got.'

After Jim did well in his fourth year at high school and wanted to go on, 'No,' his father said. 'No, lad, I'm sorry but there simply isn't the money. I need you here. It costs too damn much even for casual hands. None of those books can teach you how to run a farm.'

Although he'd wanted to answer back, to say that even without books nothing much would help in the drought years, he shut up, wishing there'd been a mother to keep things in line, like the other kids had. He recalled a period of inexplicable howling doglike grief from his father that had lasted a week, though it had seemed to him then like a year.

Remembering now, Randler wondered if the old

place had clawed stigmata on his father and himself, branded them.

A year or so after his father died he had married a city girl he met at the Brisbane Show. The marriage lasted two years, until he returned late one afternoon from the paddocks in the hot angry weather before Christmas to find she had packed up and gone. There was no note.

Why hadn't he sold up and moved when his father died – a disgruntled seventy-year-old who'd retained the picky perfectionism of his younger years but without the ability to realise it. No money, no rain, and a weight of years. Jim Randler still heard his father's last words: 'Sorry, son. I never did make you that second raft.' The old man's eyes had lit up for a minute as the words trickled out between his drying lips.

Enslaved by habit, that was it. Routine kept him going, thoughtlessly as it were. His heart wasn't in it. He craved a more detailed landscape than these flattened plains, this uncomplicated sky.

The morning he woke to decision, the sky was a drained skin with rags of cirrus peeling away to the coast.

He ticked off the components of freedom. He had sold off his land, his stock, the two farm horses, both sheepdogs – whose presence he missed more than he liked to admit. He kept Cracker, the house bitser he'd had for seven years. There was only the farmhouse and shed squatting on their few acres up from the creek. Free, he told himself.

But he was not. Driven by compulsion and that dream maggot of his youth, he drove his rattler of a truck on the long bitumen run east and reached Rockhampton in the early afternoon where he booked into a run-down hotel that gazed sluggish over the sluggish river, a pub with a sprinkling of elderly boarders as tired as he. Exhausted he might have been but he was filled also with a strange exultation. There was an inner fire to be stoked.

First he visited boatsheds along the river and asked prices. Everything was exorbitantly expensive. One boat-shed owner admitted that Randler could build what he wanted himself for half the price. The boatshed would, the man told him, supply a custom-built keel, all the planking he needed. What exactly was he after?

Randler didn't know. He was furnishing a dream. A sloop, the man at the boatshed suggested, one mast, two sails. We can fit an outboard any time. 'I want a cabin,' Randler told the man, who was a muscular giant with a sad, used face, not given to many words but a lot of thinking, 'so I can live aboard for weeks at a time. Nothing big. A bunk and a bit of a galley.'

'Twenty-one, twenty-five footer,' suggested the

boatshed man, another who had refused to go metric. 'Could you handle building something that big?'

'I don't know,' Randler said. 'I really don't know. What I do know is I'd rather do it myself. Feel part of it.'

'There is that,' the boatshed man agreed. He was an easy kind of fellow with honest eyes. 'Yes, there is that. We can supply plans, specifications, and like I said, all the timbers. But it's long work, mate. And it's hard. Had any experience with timber?'

Randler repressed a crazy impulse to tell him about the raft, that nagger failure he had yet to correct. Even if he could have afforded the overpriced yachts or launches that were on sale, he wanted no other man's dream.

He had remained a fortnight in town, waiting for plans and working sketches. The boatshed man became a friend and sometimes they drank together in the evenings. 'Boats are love affairs,' Cherry Cole said. 'Won't let you go. I know.' He had stared down into his glass and gone silent.

'Love affairs,' Randler repeated as he set about putting up stocks and cradles back in his own shed for the skeleton frame of his mistress. He would purge all memories of that almost forgotten partner. The work was hard. An oak keel, hog pieces and kelson, he'd decided, and kauri for planking. The timber was stacked along one wall of the shed. He had a basic set of tools to which he kept adding: clamps, a rebate plane, a jig for his borers. Cole had offered to drive out one weekend and help with the setting up and though Randler was touched, tempted, he kept insisting he wanted to do it alone. Despite that, his friend appeared unexpectedly one early Sunday a month later, a slab of beer in the back of his ute, a lot of advice in his head.

'Not bad,' Cole commented, surveying the keel set up on the stocks. 'Not bad at all.' He ran an inquisitive and admiring finger down the curve of the wood. Already Randler had the hogs and kelson in place and was ready to begin work on the stem. 'Look, I'm sorry for barging out without warning, but I wondered how you were going. Wanted to help if I could.'

'Not barging. I'm pleased. Come on up to the house and have a beer.'

Although Randler, used to solitariness, was uncomfortable with guests, he made a bed up for Cole on the verandah and played the uneasy host. The friendly interest on his visitor's face cheered as they faced each other across the bachelor dinner of chops and potato he served up.

'You remind me of someone,' Randler finally said. There was a beach nearly fifty years away, a beach and a kindly man who'd taught him to row. He talked about that time while they drank their tea.

129

'That was my uncle,' Cole said, grinning. 'A great old character, eh. Died a few years back. Eighty, by God, and still out there fishing, nagging me in the shed, telling me how to do it.'

They had parted the next morning, with Cole's offers of further help stubbornly declined. Yet it took the best part of six months for the skeleton of the sloop to take form and then another six to fit the planking, each day from sunup to sundown filled with problems of scarfing, treating fayed surfaces, waiting for adhesives to set. He worked with hour-long fanaticism, only pausing to brew up tea on the spirit lamp he kept in the shed. He was drunk on the smell of freshly planed timber as much as the salt-tingling tides that washed across his heart. He'd long forgotten the paddocks, the sheep, the crop planting that had been the Calvary of his years. He had smashed down the habits of a lifetime and burst through into a visionary place that might or might not become the real world. He wouldn't entertain for a moment the possibility that it might not.

It was getting there that counted.

He still went to the pub on Friday evenings and by now the whole town knew of his project, humouring old Jim because they thought he was going a bit round the twist. But they no longer asked about it. No one said any more, How's it going, mate? After the first year, when the town had weaselled out his secret and he felt compelled to talk about it, he'd known he was becoming a bore. Perhaps an eccentric, he eventually hoped with pride. Eccentricity was safer, more tolerable. Small towns, he'd learnt long ago, cherished their oddballs.

He downed his beer, nodded around the group, laughed at the right moments, and like a man obsessed with a woman thought of his sloop and its small bunk-room, savouring in retrospect the fragrance of wood and spar varnish. Another six months ('No thanks, Clem, no time for another.') he would be fitting the deck planking, hatchway, and thinking about whether to work on a timber mast or take Cole's advice and settle for a light-weight aluminium alloy.

'It's quicker,' Cole said. 'You're not getting any younger, mate.'

'Let me think about it.'

He didn't know what he would have done without Cole, who persuaded him finally to let him handle the haulage to the coast at the right time and to fit an outboard and its cable and a tiller. He was seeing the end at last; that light on a purple horizon began to hit him in the eyes.

It was towards the end of his second year working on the boat that Howie Briceland's youngest boy, Toff, a devious fourteen, began hanging around. Toff was a five-day boarder at a school in Rockhampton but on his weekends home he started appearing at the shed door, in spankingly creased shorts and designer T-shirt, poking a polite head round after a tentative knocking to make himself irresistibly invitable, wide-eyed with laddish curiosity.

'Gee, Mr Randler,' he'd enthused on that first day, but careful not to overdo it, 'it looks great. Really great! I hope you don't mind me coming over. Dad said something about it and I could hear all the work going on when I was up in the top paddock. I wondered if you might need a hand.'

Randler looked up from his sanding machine and something in the directness of those spangled eyes forced him to switch off the power and remove his earmuffs.

'What's that? What did you say?'

Toff smiled. All teeth and chirrup.

Gotcha!

He became a bit of a pest. He would turn up early on weekend mornings, ruining Randler's leisurely pot of tea and toast, sustenance for the rest of the day until his scrap evening meal. Randler didn't know how to turn him away without offence. He had built the framework of the small cabin by now and was busy fixing laminates to the studs. The passion of the dream had such force that even after working day-long in a heat-lashed shed he left off reluctantly, cooking dinner with the mental resolution of one knowing he had to fuel himself for more work, greater effort. What I will need, he imagined as he turned chops in the pan, is this and this and this.

Already he was in the boat and sailing.

The chops burned.

Another month. Two. The town was filled with term-end kids hanging about the one milk bar/café, bored witless. Toff skirted the fringes of the group.

During the school vacation he dropped in on Randler daily, his busy eyes watching with absorption while a small unrepressed smile plucked his mouth askew, play-ing a tune he would block with a casual hand, a casual cough, as he plunged fingers into his hair to rumple kid-fashion those knock-'em-dead blond curls.

'Won't be long now, hey, Mr Randler? You'll soon be off into the wide blue yonder.'

The boy was balked by the man's silent absorption. The old fart hadn't even looked up.

'Will you be taking anyone? Won't you be lonely?'

The questions were hardly worth answers. Randler kept working away at the coaming round the hatch.

'But won't you?' Toff persisted.

Finally Randler glanced across. 'I've been on my own so long, lad, I've got to like it.' He wished the little bugger would push off. No, he didn't need help but hadn't the kid better get home to help his old man with the chores? Didn't he have a holiday assignment?

'I've done it,' Toff told him with a suitably self-deprecatory smirk. 'I'm pretty smart, actually, Mr Randler. Top of my form. Dad reckons I ought to be a lawyer. What do you think?'

'I don't think,' Randler said, needled, 'except about this. Just let me get on with it, lad, there's a good chap.'

But Toff was back after a cooling-off period of a week, just to see how it was going.

'Boy!' he said, his quick eyes registering some kind of admiration – it worked on all his teachers – his fingers stroking the hull. 'You're doing a beautiful job.'

'I am, am I?' Randler couldn't help succumbing a little to such overt flattery. He gave Toff a grin. He found his hand stroking the sheer as well, caressing, sensing the satin of the wood enter his own skin and pulse up through his arm. He smiled and Toff caught the smile and held it.

'Great job,' the boy enthused. 'Great, great job. Ex-cell-ent!'

The swelter days of December. Almost ready for Cole's haulage to the coast and the fitting out of sails and outboard. An emergency feature, that last, he kept telling himself, Cole kept telling him, for tricky harbour entrances, for mooring, for those landfalls of the mind.

He preferred to think of his sails engorged with wind, taking him out on the roadsteads, a dancer about the islands studding the littoral. Always a dreamer. Sometimes, sagging exhausted back at the house after a ten-hour day in the shed, he could smile wryly as he realised his status as an armchair mariner, stuffed with Masefield but little theory, a schoolboy reading of coral islands and buccaneers and no practice beyond the half-dozen visits he had made in his adult years back to the same beach, the same lagoon, to find the elderly couple moved on but the dinghy rental business still there.

The new owner had encouraged him to hire a small skiff and he had skated across flecked glass, intoxicated with both the sound and the silence of air and water, the noises of space eaten by wind. It was then he knew what he wanted most but doubted there would ever be the opportunity; he could see no escape from the farm, the heat dust poverty of his life.

But he'd changed that. He'd made the break.

Another week. Two. Some final spit and polish to the tiny cabin. A bunk. A cooking bench.

Toff loitered round the edges of Saturday morning.

'Almost there, hey?'

Randler grunted as he fiddled with rudder and

135

pintles, not looking up, keeping his eye to the particulars of the business.

'Let's come on up, Mr Randler,' Toff pleaded, admiring. 'Let's have a look at the cabin.'

So he'd given in, simmering in his own pride, watching the kid peering, feeling, even cheekily flopping on the narrow bunk.

'What about the mast and sails?'

'They're being fitted down the coast. I'll be there.' He thought it was like assisting at a religious rite. 'I'll be there doing my bit.'

'And then you'll be off, yeah?' Toff rolled off the bunk, climbed up the hatchway and stood for a moment on the deck, his eyes raking man, boat, shed, in a dizziness of envy. 'Hey,' he said. 'How about that!'

He ambled off, looking back once to see if the old geezer watched, but he was bent over the deck again, fussing around the rudder housing, and the whole of a turned around Saturday scalded the boy's mind as he went down towards the creek, dodging through the scrub past Massig's house and heading towards the footbridge and the road into town.

Yes, she was a beauty, old Randler decided, standing back to gloat over his clinker-built love. Nearly three years of work had gone into it: the primitive steam box he'd built for the planking, the fixing with clenched nails, carving the rebates, the seemingly endless coats of varnish. He smiled at his passion. It was to be rigged fore and aft and he had attached a bowsprit for the jib stay. Each morning now he took his mug of tea to the shed to stand sipping and looking, sipping and looking.

Cherry Cole had promised to be up to shift her to his workshed near Yeppoon within the fortnight. Randler would wait there with the boat, rather like a father outside a maternity ward, expectant, letting the surgeon fingers of Cole make the final adjustments and bring it to birth, full term, launched into the silky tide of the marina. He hadn't yet decided on a name but something suggested *Vagabond*, which seemed hackneyed enough but held its own memories and harmonics of those memories. There was a poem by Stevenson they'd all chanted on afternoons in the classroom, staring at the chalk-streaked blackboard, the globe, the pictures of the Barron in flood, the aerial view of the Whitsunday Passage, and outside the windows the sagging pepper trees blocking the dry curves of the seemingly endless sheep paddocks.

He leaned back on a bench in the shed and lit a cigarette. Words that kid of Briceland's had uttered kept coming back and fanning resentment. 'All the same, Mr Randler, it's kind of out of date, isn't it? Like *clinker*! Everything's fibreglass now. Even concrete.'

'There's nothing as beautiful as timber,' he'd said. 'Anyway, lad, I'm out of date too. Almost passed my use-by date.'

But he put the thought aside in the steady lapping of water against the bow.

Another two weeks and he would lock the house, whistle his old dog Cracker onto the front seat of his truck and they'd hit the road and the high seas together. Well, not the high seas. A journey up to the Whitsundays for a start, maybe as far as the Cape if he found he was handling things right.

That night he stayed late in the shed, putting finishing touches to the tiny cabin – the cooking bench, the storage cupboards – touching up the painted surfaces with the care, he thought, of a woman making up her face. Cole had promised to fit a small gas cooker and fridge. Not that he would need much. He planned to live off the sea. When he returned to the house he fell asleep almost at once, to dream of fish fresh from the water, tasting of salt and the sea gardens.

Now he had reached the end of his labour, the days dragged. He rang Cole and asked if he could bring the date forward. 'Only by a couple of days,' Cole told him, his voice frayed by distance and bad connection. 'I'll be up on Monday.' When Randler replaced the phone in its cradle it seemed that he had erased fifty years of grinding farm work in one beautifully timed decision that would take him from Drylands to waterlands in a second. At night admiralty charts fluttered from uncurled sleeping fingers to the floor beside his bed, frightening Cracker who grunted and lurched away to his usual corner in the living-room.

Three more days. Impatience was making him despise – that was the word, though it shamed him – the farm that had sucked so many decades from him; reject the townsfolk whom he knew too well, the street of sun-dried fly-struck stores, the sheer languor of service, a languor he had once admired as a countryman's quirk that set him apart from the money-grubbers of city canyons, a languor – the *manyana* principle he called it – that he had practised himself until now.

No more. He slept dream-filled in hope.

Toff's dad was a councillor, fat with graft, expense accounts unvouchable for, owner of one of the larger grazing properties now swollen by Randler's sell-off, owner of Drylands' one hardware store where he rarely gave dockets for cash sales but siphoned off the week's takings for household expenses, neatly obviating earnings declarations for tax purposes. ('Christ, Win, everyone does it.')

Onya, Pop!

Toff hung about quietly, shadowlike, ears alert when

139

the olds discussed business, bickered over debts, hopped into the neighbours with petty censure, planned financial coups. He'd early learned to appreciate the finer points of rorting and living well. Yet despite his approval of parental scams, he resented his parents themselves for his having, in a gloomily ripening adolescence, to fend off the jibes of schoolmates whose own parents were aware, or victims, or less successful. In fact he loathed the older generation his parents moved in: buddies from properties farther out, coastal businessmen and their wives who came up for loud drunken weekends and planned development along the seaboard. And he loathed even more the generation beyond that: smells, wrinkles, contused veins, the staggers, jowls, guts, curved frail bones, plastic munchers, word-gropers. Gross!

And oldsters had everything in a way. Rights of passage. Small authorities. Large authorities. Even when they couldn't remember, the stupid old bastards, the name of their local bank manager, the man who'd leased the next property out but one, the names of his friends – he didn't have many – they could remember to the last piddling detail the proscriptions demanded by custom, all the half-pint tyrannies adults felt free to impose by virtue of their age.

The plan he had been fermenting during sleepless nights of the last school term ripened as the full moon fined down to its last quarter. He'd come home that weekend with a lousy note from his form teacher who'd found him cheating during the maths paper in the yearly exams. Stuff 'em, he thought, wriggling under the hot sheets. Stuff the lot of them. He didn't want to go back to that dump next year, anyway. His poncy father had raised eyebrows and said it was about time, anyhow, he came back to help on the property. The only use an expensive school like his had, his father pronounced, waggling a spoon for emphasis over the apple crumble, was to make connections. The right connections. Toff hadn't made any.

He shifted his hatred out from the centre. Bishop's gambit. He had to whip up reasons for his next move. He recalled the indifference of old Randler to his earnest youthful presence, the rejection of proffered help, the selfishness of the old bugger, yes, the sheer bloody mean-ness, when it came down to it, of refusing to share even the sawdust and shavings of his dream.

Resentment made him feel better. He smiled in the dark, lying awake waiting for the olds to hit the sack, not to listen in to erotic tumblings, for they were so rare he regarded his parents as neuters, but to hear the heavy snoring of the old man and the lighter, regular breathing of mumsie entwined in God knows what dreams of profit and loss, a snooze duet that would make it possible for him to lever up his casement window and head into mindless midnight.

He checked his watch. Twelve-fifteen. Surely old Randler would be asleep by now.

Gently he slid out of bed and padded across to turn the key in his bedroom door against outside intrusion. He pulled on black joggers and beanie and let himself out the window into a fragrance of bruised geraniums.

Stock-still. Waiting.

Toff felt a bit of a pro. He had a small history of petty crime that had never been brought home to him. There was that little matter of the primary school out at Drylands Creek, a trashed convenience store not far from his own school, an unexplained paint job on a war memorial in downtown Rocky. Not that he stole things. The kicks didn't come from that. He was above stealing, he decided with savage pride. It was something deeper, a tiny fuse of hatred that burned away like a pilot light. He'd never had a girl. He'd tried. He still remembered the laughter.

Over the house lawn, now, through the paddocks and past the imbecile stares of drowsy cows to the creek that led up past Massig's place and twisted in behind Randler's property. There wasn't much left, his dad having bought most of it. Randler's home paddock was a mess of unslashed weed and the beginnings of scrub growth that Toff knew clump by clump.

He crouched behind a stand of wattle, from where he could see the dark hump of Randler's house and the higher ridge of the shed. In the farmhouse one window stamped a yellow rectangle against night-plush and Toff waited, chewing his nails in fury that the old sod was still up. He wished he smoked, like his classmates, but there was a manic puritanism that drove him into mental violences that had no connection with torpor or ease or the small carnal comforts the other kids talked about. He never masturbated. He was relieved by convulsive dreams that left him drained. He never nicked drinks from his father's stocked cellar. He perfected a vile sterility.

Sometimes he surprised himself with the rampage of his wishes. A military plane manoeuvring from its coastal base and leaving an upward-lengthening contrail across the passive blue once swept him unexpectedly behind the controls in a downward, ever-accelerating plunge to the miraculous, longed-for whump-explosion-oblivion. When he returned from the verandah he could hardly swallow his breakfast cereal.

'Did you see that plane?' he had asked his dad, hidden behind the *Red Plains Gazette*.

'Eat your breakfast, lad.'

'But did you?'

His father rose, made a face at his wife and took tea and paper into another room.

Toff could only grin.

He grinned now in the patchy dark, revolving in his mind every aspect of his forward move, every leap of his backward flight, knowing each hide of scrub like familiars, every secret waterhole in the dying creek that made the faintest of gasping sounds to his left as it staggered over a small rockfall on its way to Massig's.

The moon sliver wasted away and the window in Randler's house suddenly became a rectangle of black. Still Toff waited, chewing on a grass stalk, waiting until the stalk was a tasteless string that cut at the edges of his tongue. He spat a silent slobber of grass and saliva and lay back listening to the earth tick. Nothing disturbed him, neither rustle nor slither. He became grounded, literally, earth-merged, closing his eyes until another hour went by. His watch said two-thirty before he began a cautious progress to the shed, armed with the aids in his pockets, the kerosene-soaked fire starters, the matches.

Briefly he wondered about the dog. It slept inside, he knew. He'd asked about that innocently enough weeks ago. Silence was everything.

The old fool hadn't bothered padlocking the shed. This was a town where they still believed nothing happened. Didn't they know times had changed? He eased the door open and tiptoed up to the hulk of the boat where it slumbered on its scaffold-trestles imagining the sea.

This would be different, Toff decided, not like that crummy one-teacher-school job where he had merely chucked stuff about. He laid his fire starters in strategic spots in the belly of the cabin, like white nougat decorating the cupboard skirtings, the bunk. Sorry, mate, he whispered and grinned again. He scattered wood shavings over the decking and soaked them with petrol from the can Randler kept in a corner of the shed. Not enough, he regretted, and nosed about the walls of the building with his pencil-flash until he found cans of paint-stripper and methylated spirits.

Quick! He had to be quick!

A dousing. A baptism.

He wanted to yell aloud 'I name thee *Firebird*' as he lit the matches here and here and here, wanted to stay for the orgasm of blaze but watched only the first whoop of flame before running out into the still night and heading for the far paddock where he stood to watch the fire tango across the windows of the shed, standing entranced, his sneakers soaked by early dew. 'Cop that, old man,' he whispered, stepping back and back, hugging his inward scream of pleasure, his eyes reflecting fire, stepping back until he was absorbed by trees, while the flames mounted and fattened and played with old Randler's boat and rolled it on its moorings and hissed like waves.

Randler was woken by his fretter of a heeler whimpering and pawing at the bedclothes. He grumbled a little and tossed about before sitting up. 'What is it, boy?' he muttered sleepily, wanting to roll over. The dog persisted, snuffling and barking in sharp isolated yelps. Beyond his bedroom window Randler glimpsed through sleep-heavy eyes a fearful orange glow. Oh God! he thought. God! He stumbled to the verandah and could see through the side windows of the shed the wild surf of light breaking and surging in a rising tide. As he watched, a window blew out.

He raced from the house in his pyjamas, down the paddock, feet catching on grass tufts, heart jumping and battering his ribcage. His throat tightened so that he could hardly breathe, gulping for air across his dried tongue. A fearsome screech began in the pit of his bowels and rose, gathering despair and rage, up through his throat to emerge in a wolf howl that bawled its frightful grief across the landscape.

It was hopeless. He knew it was hopeless. It was too late. The side walls of the shed were beginning to catch. Yet despite that, almost automatically he grabbed a hose that was hooked to the pump from the creek and began soaking the doorway and the walls around before moving in. He was sobbing and hating at the one time.

The heat was appalling. But even then, even with the stink of singeing he could now smell from his thinning hair, he moved forward and kicked open the door in some kind of idiot optimism.

There, cradled in light, festooned with glittering streamers of fire, the boat, a glowing hulk like a phoenix that would never rise from its ashes, shuddered and rocked. Stupidity and desperation directed the hose at it, and slabs of ruined planking crumbled from the impact of water and fell to the floor.

For a while he kept the hose playing on his dream, futilely – the tears he couldn't shed – and after a time, beyond even the possibility of preserving a minimum of it, he went out into the pre-dawn grey, turned off the tap and walked back to the house. There was nothing that could be done. The three-year serial was over.

'The hell with it!' he said aloud.

He began to toss clothes into a bag. The anger would come later in a surge that would take all will away. He must leave before then. 'Finished,' he kept muttering, and heard his voice like a stranger's. 'Finished.'

He picked up his bag and with the dog trotting after went out to the truck.

Eclipse.

Beyond thought.

Beyond anything but the physical moment.

He got up behind the wheel, whistled the dog into the seat beside him, started the motor and swung off down the lane ruts that would take him to the road, to the east, to the inevitable sea.

MEANWHILE . . .

'There are people called Murphy moving in,' Paddy Locke had said to her as she paid for her morning paper. 'Now at last I will be able to discuss Teilhard de Chardin.'

Janet had hidden an unbelieving smile. 'Fossils or the Omega point?' she asked blandly as she slipped the paper into a plastic bag. Was she actually hearing these words in Drylands?

'Well!' miffed Paddy Locke said. 'Well! How about *you*!'

Paddy Locke lived on the outskirts of town in an abandoned weatherboard she had bought more that eight years ago. 'Driven here,' she confessed at various meetings of inquisitive country women's groups and show association strategy assemblies, 'by city prices.' Everyone had nodded wisely but could prise no further information from her.

Her age hovered between fifty and sixty. There had been a Mr Locke, it was deduced from throwaway oblique references she made when her guard was down. She was a slight woman with glasses and wispy tawny hair worn in an untidy bun. Apart from a horticultural frenzy in her front garden which she had turned by some inner magic into a denseness of shrub and flower that caused surprised neighbourly comment, she had been a shadowy figure in the township, one of those characters who enter stage left and almost immediately exit stage right after some trifling announcement about dinner or a possible World War III. But in the last four years she had suddenly come forward as a force agitating for a branch of the Red Plains library to be established in town. No one was interested.

What's great about these godforsaken holes, Janet decided next morning, leaning over her small balcony and watching the place rub its eyes and start to wake up, are the oddballs. They stand out. You meet them. They enrich. No. More. They furbish the day.

Was she one herself?

She recalled her mother's frequently repeated warning about the inability to read. Mother had added riders from time to time: 'It's like foot-binding in China. Of course,' she had gone on, stuffed with political zeal and irritation, 'the more illiterates the easier for governments to supply slave labour to the wealthy. Think of that.'

She had had a bad night in her small flat above the

152

newsagency. The close tin roof had creaked and groaned as the night air cooled it, and at one stage she could have sworn she heard movement at the back door of the shop. Fumbling her way downstairs in the dark, not wanting to switch lights on and warn intruders off, she had twisted an ankle when she missed the bottom step and crashed into a chair. While she stood there wincing, biting back cries, she heard the quick flip-flop of running feet across her yard, then the scramble as a body hoisted itself over the paling fence.

Imagination, she wanted to assure herself. Briefly she wondered how Paddy Locke coped alone. She should ask her in for tea. She should call. She should do something about the proposed library committee which, she admitted, could destroy her small business. But then – cynical laugh – she had no business. Not for books. Those were the moments when she wanted to pack up and leave. But the same reason that had driven Paddy Locke here kept her entrapped. That and ultimately a peculiar sense of belonging.

She looked back at the table where she worked in the evenings, a mess of paper breaking like surf against her typer. The mechanics of storytelling bothered her. It didn't rush from her fingers. Should it? She reserved a certain contempt for the lavishing of detail. It was better for readers to frolic with their own assumptions from the words spoken, the deeds done. Exercise those minds, she thought, citing Mother who had managed to align mathematical conclusions with character assessment. 'Darling,' she had advised her teenage daughter, 'always watch mouths. The angles. They're the giveaway.'

Should she try for a little Nabokov rococo? Sentences as long and meandering with tributary clauses as Faulkner's Mississippi? A touch of Hemingway minimalism?

She could persist only. Tap, tap, and tap.

She thought of Ted in those months before he died. He'd been too weak to hold up the paper, balance a book in his wobbling hands. 'Can't manage it, love,' he'd said. 'Give us the local gossip.' So she'd read him the more interesting bits from the *Gazette* and watched with pride and pleasure when he asked, 'Give me a look. I want to see that last bit again.' She'd always left the room then on some thin excuse like putting the kettle on, but would come back to find him bent over the flattened paper, smiling at a paragraph that described local disaster: the tea marquee collapsing at the picnic races and blotting two members of parliament, a Japanese land developer and the shire clerk for half an hour. Or front-page town outrage over Benny Shoforth's housing struggle with the local council. Bit of a boong, they all said contemptuously in pub bars, in shops. Touch of the old tarbrush! Bloody fuss over nothing.

Did these things matter? Did they not?

'Ted,' she said aloud. 'I want to stop, but it's a diary of my days. In a way. In a way.'

TRUMPED

The bicycle. The stiff wire masts fore and aft with a small triangular flag as a warning to cars. The light trailer cart hitched behind into which Benny Shoforth could pack his weekly shopping.

'Here comes the crazy old geezer!' they'd said for the first few months of Benny's odd-looking transport. Laughs in the pub. Schoolkid whistles and chiacks and later a terrorising by skateboards doing wheelies and figures of eight around him as he pedalled past. By the end of the year, though, they took it as normal. 'Pity more of us don't do it,' Clem said to a group of drinkers at the Lizard. 'Think of what we'd save in petrol.'

Benny Shoforth had lived for the last ten years in a broken-down shack on a five-acre patch outside town. A spare fellow given to silence. Sixty-five? Seventy? Somewhere way back there'd been a cross-cultural fornication. One of the white pastoralists had spent the lonely weeks of his wife's annual holiday in Brisbane establishing friendly relations with the half-caste house-girl whom he sacked before his wife returned. When Benny was born his father was active in getting the fringe dwellers moved on and Benny, under the protection of the Act, was carried off to a reserve outside Brisbane where he grew up without knowing any parentage at all.

You'd have to peer closely to spot that touch of tar-brush. Was it the deep-set quality of his eyes? The bony angles of his profile? The merest – the very merest – driftwood tint to the skin?

No one was ever certain. And because of that, no one was ever certain how to treat him. Was he one of them, the skin-privileged, or did he deserve dismissive contempt? The very unsureness gave offence. In the narrow social circle of the town the men were frightened of putting a foot wrong. It didn't worry the women nearly as much. The men formed a tighter blokeship club whose unwritten codes were more fiercely adhered to than those of their wives. All the town women who had had dealings with Benny Shoforth were impressed by his good manners, his assistance with shopping bags when they were overloaded, his quietly tipped hat on passing. Sometimes he did a spot of gardening to help out when husbands were away and his polite declining of offered cups of tea later with 'I've got to be getting back' had them flummoxed and impressed. He seemed to pocket the payments they made with reluctance. Often he refused payment. 'Glad to help out,' he'd say.

How the hell do you deal with that?

Disaster hit Benny when the town council at Red Plains warned him they'd have to sell up his property for unpaid rates. He was on the old-age pension now, and the payments were beyond him. He'd always managed with odd jobs after he became too old to work on the sheep properties as general dogsbody and shed hand. Years before, after he'd run away from the reserve in the south, he'd got a job as a fettler on the railways and worked the length of the coastal line, putting money by for a guessed at future. This meant marriage in his late twenties to another part-white, a young woman with a dash of island blood who'd been at Yarrabah and was working as cook on a cane farm near Eungella. He craved a base, a sense of permanency. He wanted children of his own. The government was still snatching children, but not with the same merciless intensity of twenty years before. If he managed to get a little house, he thought, and prove his independence and his ability to look after his family, they might leave him alone.

But they had had no children and when Mellie died ten years ago, Benny decided he would go back to the place he knew as his origins. It was easier to discover now.

He was thirteen before he found out where his mother had come from. While he was still at the reserve he became friendly with one of the older men who had been rounded up from the same place. 'Your mum's still around,' the old man told him. 'Gone to work down Ipswich way for a bit. Then she gone out Charleville, house cook on one of them big stations.'

The knowledge ate at him.

At fifteen he'd run off from the fencing job he'd been given on a property near Gatton and walked and walked and hitched rides out to the end of the south-western line, walking mostly, because no one wanted to pick up a stranger with that faint sepia blush about the skin even if he did look no more than a kid. The old man back at the reserve had told him his mother's name. 'Called Jilly,' he said. 'Not her tribal name, eh. One them mission blokes call her.'

Benny wandered along the near-empty wide dusty streets of that town at the end of the line. He felt noticed, noticeable, until he ran into three black men drinking on the footpath outside a run-down pub. It was late afternoon, the sun slanting bright diagonals across parked trucks, pepper trees, the tin roofs of houses. The men were still sober enough to listen. They offered him a drink. He shook his head. 'Where you stayin?' they asked. He didn't know. And even as he didn't know he saw the big copper car pulling in and the man getting out and strolling towards the group, casual over the inner threat.

'Who's this then, eh?' the copper asked.

'Cousin,' one of the men said quickly. 'Benny's down from Augathella, see his uncle.'

'Bullshit,' the copper said amiably. 'You blokes get along now. You've had enough of the old piss. Time you were getting back to camp before the wives get shitty.'

They laughed. They were supposed to laugh and the copper was appeased by this appreciation of his wit. 'Okay, now. On your way.' He stood there, a burly giant with a not quite smile on his sun-brick face, until they had turned and begun to walk along the back streets out of town.

At the camp down on the riverbank they gave Benny tucker and let him pitch his swag on the edge of the campfire. He told them that he was looking for his mother, that he'd heard she worked on one of the stations up along the Warrego. Jilly, he said. Jilly.

'She still there,' they told him. 'Bin there long time, eh, but still workin. Out long that big place near Warrego Crossin. She get big surprise, when you turn up.'

That night he slept at the camp and in the morning washed himself down in one of the waterholes along the river. One of the women had some damper going when he got back and a tin mug of treacle-black tea to wash it down. There were only seven of them in the camp, the three men he had met, their wives, and a small girl of two who hid behind her mother and watched him with one dark eye peeping round.

'She's a pretty kid,' Benny couldn't help saying.

'Your mum still pretty,' the woman said.

'Is she?'

'Don't talk much, but. She bin all quiet since we know. Won't talk when she see us. Jus work, eh?'

Benny rubbed damper crumbs from the front of his shirt, gulped the last of his tea and picked up his swag.

'Better be goin,' he said. 'Thanks.'

They looked at him in silence and then one of the men said to let them know when he was on the way back through, let them know how he was doing. He nodded and raised one hand and set off along the track they pointed out.

Benny Shoforth lay awake on his camp stretcher in the old house he would have to leave and remembered that meeting.

He didn't want to remember. It hurt too much.

There he'd been, a gangly fifteen-year-old, walking up to the gates of the big property, heading along the home track wondering when the buildings would appear. They must have been a mile in, hidden by coolabah and gidgee. A pair of blue heelers started barking as he came up the last stretch, racing around him as if they were going to pen him in, and then he was aware of a man approaching from a paddock on his right, a slim young fellow riding a handsome bay and whistling the dogs off.

'Looking for someone?' the man had asked. Not friendly. Not unfriendly. A warning-off sound. A boss voice. Benny hesitated before answering. He had learned early never to tell too much. 'Have to see Jilly,' he said. 'Got a message.'

'I can give her that.'

'It's personal,' Benny told him.

'Well, now.' The young fellow's eyebrows lifted. His horse was beginning to fidget and dance about. 'Not too personal, I hope.' Suddenly he grinned. 'Straight ahead, then turn right round the side of the homestead. She should be in the kitchen out the back.'

'Thanks, mister.' Benny set off walking again, swag hitched over his shoulder. He could sense the man's eyes following him as he trudged up the last hundred yards towards the low-verandahed building that was tucked back behind dried-out lawn and grevillea. He forced

163

himself not to look around, kept his head down, watching his feet, and then he heard the horse trotting up behind and the man drew alongside and waited while he turned right and went round the side of the house, stepping carefully along the gravel paths till he came to the extension built out from the main building. As he walked up the steps onto the verandah he did turn, and saw the man on his horse reined in and still watching.

The kitchen screen doors let him see right into the big room where two women were working over a sink with piles of dishes. One of them. His mum.

He tapped on the frame of the screen and the older one looked over. She was a big black woman with a wide face and bright eyes. 'What you want?' she asked.

'Want to speak to Jilly.'

'Well, here she is. Right here.'

The other woman put down her dishmop and walked across to the door. She was young. Well, younger than he thought she'd be. He stared at her through the mesh of fly-wire. Light-skinned, small. Yeah, pretty, he could see that. Suddenly he didn't know what to say. There weren't the words. All those words he'd learnt at the reserve school. He could read, write. He knew bits of history, geography that had been drummed into him in that hot primitive classroom. If he shut his eyes he could still see the slates, the inkwells, the big map on the wall and a fly-specked picture of a man and woman from England somewhere. The teacher had said they were the king and queen. That hadn't meant anything. He could figure out sums. He could smell that room and the kids wriggling at the desks around him, their feet shifting and scraping along the floorboards. Now everything was gone.

He stammered something that didn't sound like words and went silent.

Then there was the sound of feet treading along the verandah and the man from the horse was standing right behind him, checking his property, his servants.

'Young feller says he's got a message for you, Jilly.' The man stood so close, Benny could feel his body-heat, smell sweat.

'I'll give him a cuppa,' the big woman said. 'That orright, boss?'

'Okay,' the man said. 'That might loosen him up. And then you'd better get him on his way.' He swung about and his feet went thump thump thump down the stairs and out into the yard.

'You better come on in,' the big woman said. So he pushed the screen door back and went in and sat at one end of the kitchen table while the woman poured tea into a mug.

He didn't know how to start. He took a sip and put the mug down and looked from one woman to the other.

The big one smiled. 'C'mon! We ain't got all day, boy. What's your name?'

'Benny,' he said. Then it came in a rush. 'Benny's the name they gave me at the reserve. And Jilly's my mum.'

The kitchen fell silent. The kettle's spluttering died away and Jilly put down her dishmop and came over to the table and lowered herself into a chair. She stared at the boy. He stared back and then dropped his eyes.

'You gammon, eh?' the big woman said.

'No gammon.' Benny's feet shifted under the table, sought for and found the rungs of his chair.

'Jilly don't say much,' the big woman said. She turned and looked at her companion. 'Could be?' she asked.

Jilly looked down and nodded.

Then she spoke, her voice small and uncertain. She asked where the reserve was, said she'd been taken there too but put in the women's section. A half-wail broke from her mouth. Benny became frozen where he sat. Her pain was his. She'd asked and asked to see him, she said, and then after a few months they'd sent her out to work on a property near Marburg. Then later the boss moved her on to this place.

She put one thin brown hand across the table and touched Benny's fingers. 'You man now,' she said. 'All them years, eh?'

Then she got up and came round the table and put her arms around him and he could smell the dusky dusty smell of her and felt her thin body shake as she hugged him, shake and shake.

166

'Tell me,' he said, 'how did it happen? Who was he, my father?'

Jilly lifted her head and stared over Benny's shoulders, her eyes blank or filled with unwanted memories.

'She got busted,' the big woman interrupted. 'Boss-busted. Man called Briceland out Red Plains way. Jilly was housegirl there, helpin. Me too. Our mob lived down by the creek and had jobs now and then, fencin, herdin. The boss's wife was away at the coast and he busted Jilly. Kept at her till his wife come back. Jilly was only a kid, twelve, thirteen. Soon as he see what's happenin, he get rid of the evidence, eh?'

She laughed without mirth and went back to the stove and began stirring something in a large saucepan.

'She don't like talkin about it none.' The big woman tossed words over her shoulder. They thudded like small stones. 'She married now, one of the stockmen, Charlie Harris. They got little place on the property.'

Benny took his arms away gently from his mother and sat back in his chair and looked at her standing there, hunched over her grief. 'I got brothers?' he asked. 'Sisters?'

His mother shook her head.

She was only young, not even thirty, he estimated. He was disappointed at the lack of family. In the very marrow of him he knew family was important.

'Lissen, boy,' the woman by the stove said, 'you ask

too many questions, eh? Don't you upset her. You want the truth, that ole Briceland he so rough with her, she can't have no more kids. After you was born, the doctor feller he tell her that. I was there, see, down that same reserve, and they let her keep you a bit before they took you away to the boys' dormitory and then they bung Jilly off long with me for domestic work. That's what they call it. Not our own domestic work. Other folks'.' She went over to the sink and refilled the kettle, dumping it back angrily on the stove. Water hissed and spat on the iron hob.

'This Charlie,' Benny asked his mum, 'he good to you?'

Jilly nodded. He had to lean close to hear. 'Part white too. He understand.'

'No one understand,' the big woman said. 'No one.'

He hardly felt the stones through his worn-out sandshoes on the way back to town. His mind was a turmoil of discovery, bitterness, anger. Anger for what had happened to both of them: to his thin pretty mother, battered into silence by events she couldn't control; for himself for what he had lost.

He'd been quick and keen at the reserve school. His teacher, Mr Bussell, found him moving ahead of the others in his group, reading whatever the tattered supply of schoolbooks could offer. One day he overheard Mr Bussell say to the superintendent, 'Young Shoforth must have had a bright white daddy. He's miles ahead of the others. I think we ought to let him try for the scholarship.'

He'd pressed back behind the classroom door, hating the implication that the black bits were stupid. He waited until he heard the two men walk away across the yard and then he took a piece of chalk and wrote on the blackboard:

> I love a sunburnt country.
> The land belongs to me.
> I'd like to see the whites strung up
> From every gidgee tree.

'Stand up the boy who wrote that!' Mr Bussell said next morning. There was a long silence. Some of the older boys began to giggle.

'You will all be punished,' Mr Bussell warned. He was not a cruel man. He was simply forced to play by the rules. Secretly he was impressed by the neatness of the parody. He wouldn't have suspected anyone in this rag-tag class capable of doing it. There was only one boy who might have written those words. His eyes fixed on Benny Shoforth sitting quietly at the back of the class and for the longest of moments they looked at each other. Then Benny raised his hand.

'Yes?' Mr Bussell said.

'I did it.'

'Come out here, lad.'

Benny shuffled out to the front of the class.

'Get the duster and rub out those words.'

Benny stood there mute.

'You heard what I said, boy. Rub them out.'

No one in the room moved. In the morning heat the smell of sweat and fear, glutinous and tart, became almost palpable.

'I can't,' Benny said.

'Why not?'

'I mean them.'

Mr Bussell sighed. 'I'll have to cane you,' he said, adding, 'but you have a fine sense of scansion.'

'What's that?' Benny asked.

'Never mind,' Mr Bussell said.

He walked over to the cupboard and took out his cane and went back to the front of the room. He was hating this job, hating the tensions of the reserve, the governmental intransigence, the sheer selfish idiocy of the whole system. He'd be gone by Christmas, he vowed inwardly, and said to the skinny kid before him, 'Hold out your hand.'

He gave the offered palm the merest flick with the cane and went over to the board and erased the last two lines before turning to look at the class. Twenty eyes looked back. 'Well,' Mr Bussell commented, risking public service permanence, 'you're right about the first bit.' Then he rubbed that out too.

He didn't report the matter. The superintendent never got to hear of it. But the incident, brief as it was, bonded teacher and class and made the last months of that year more tolerable.

They didn't allow Benny to sit the scholarship exam after all, and before either the war or the year ended he ran off from the reserve and worked fencing on a run-down sheep property near Condamine. Once when he had to go to town to help pick up supplies in the property's truck, he saw Mr Bussell walk by. They looked at each other, Benny's heart jumping for fear he might be dragged back to that place he'd learned to hate, but all Mr Bussell did was smile and say, 'Hello, Benny. Don't worry, son. I haven't seen you.' Then he'd walked on without a glance and Benny's heart stopped jumping and the day grew bluer and he whistled as he stacked feed bags in the pick-up, so happy the missus said, 'What's made you chirpy all of a sudden, Benny?'

And he simply couldn't say.

Two years of this and that.

Taller. Knew more. Thought he knew more. Still had

the pocket dictionary he'd pinched from the books cupboard the day he ran away from the reserve. Sneaked it out before anyone could see and rammed it under his shirt. He wasn't sure why he'd done that but he never let go of it. Sometimes at night he'd read bits. He knew words mattered. Every so often he thought about going to look for his mum. Thought about it until finally curiosity ate him up and forced him on his way. Ate him up and ended with those words, 'No one understand.'

For a while after that he'd managed to see his mother off and on. He worked now on the railway that ran through to Brisbane and because he looked more white than black found he was paid more. When he and his mother met, nothing was able to dissolve that tundra of years that had separated them. That's what made them both weep secretly and hopelessly after each parting. In the end it seemed easier not to make that painful visit to the big homestead. Three years on he found out that his mother and Charlie had moved away and rented a poverty-spare patch outside Rockhampton. Charlie was getting by with seasonal work on the cane and pineapple farms.

Benny got a more or less permanent job in the railway yards in Rockhampton. No one worried much about his ancestry or perhaps it didn't show. He spoke differently now. Even back at the reserve his words had been losing that pidgin coloration that marked him and his people as a lesser breed. He kept to himself. Not unfriendly. Not

172

too friendly. His wife Mellie worked as a cleaner in a hotel and together they managed to save sufficient money to buy an old shack on a couple of acres outside Drylands, hoping to move there some time. Back to the start of things. His start. The dream, he had told her. It's the dream.

Now, all these decades later, he was losing that as well.

He gave up trying to sleep and went out to the kitchen and boiled up some coffee.

What was the point of mulling over all those years?

No point, really, but as a sop to loneliness.

All those stupid plans, he thought as he sat sipping his over-brewed coffee in the wideawake house, had come to nothing. They'd never had kids. Mellie had died in her late forties and his mother not long after. He had gone out to visit the old place where she and Charlie Harris had lived and found it abandoned and scrawled with spiderwebs, Charlie having cleared out for Brisbane, nursing loneliness and bereavement with the bottle.

Benny had never felt so lost.

There and then he decided to give up his job at the railway yards and move out to Drylands to try his hand at subsistence living. All he took from his mother's house was a sagging Genoa-velvet three-piece lounge suite and a picture of her and Charlie sitting on a sand hill at Yeppoon watching the ocean.

He had that picture in front of him now and ran a

fingertip over the yellowed surface that showed his mother trying to smile – he guessed she was trying to smile – and Charlie, one arm about her thin shoulders, the two of them there just staring at the panting sea. He thought it was the saddest thing he had ever seen.

If he had been honest with himself he would have admitted he had chosen Drylands as a roosting place because that was where his mother had conceived him. Wait! That was too gentle, too generous a phrase to use. Correction: where his mother had been raped by Howard Briceland's father; where Howard lived in pastoralist comfort, a big man in the district, an opinion swayer on council, a known enemy of Benny Shoforth's people.

Half-people, Benny thought, but without bitterness. He didn't know where he stood in the scale of things but he believed the only way to play the people game was to play it white way. Sometimes when he passed Briceland in Drylands, he wanted badly to say, 'I'm your brother. Your half-brother. Let's go and have a drink, mate.' With an extra-acerbic ironic stress on the 'mate'. Always he held himself in check. It was easier to turn the other cheek. It was safer. And that cheek-turning was, he discovered to his delight, often maddening.

He sat through the night in one of those old lounge chairs, waiting for the sun to come picking its way through the scrub. Give it an hour, he decided, and he'd be on the move. No use making further appeals to the

174

council. No whimpers for mercy. They'd handed him notice to quit and given him a final date to vacate the premises. That moment came with sunup. Not for him those humiliating tailpiece tussles with council heavies and police forcing him out under the eyes of a smirking real estate agent come to assess the leavings. He'd made his plans and he'd stick to them.

And after that?

He owned so little.

He looked around the room that served as kitchen and sitting-room. A small pine table and two chairs he'd picked up cheap at a fire sale in Red Plains, the lounge suite with its awful nostalgic autumn tonings, his mantel radio that worked off batteries, and half a dozen books. He slept on a fold-up camp stretcher in a small room off the kitchen, a room with one window that faced east and trapped hope each day with the rising sun. He was glad he hadn't woken there this particular morning.

He began shovelling his few spare bits of clothing into a cardboard box. Then the books: the dictionary, an atlas, a copy of Jack London's stories, Hemingway's *The Old Man and the Sea* ('I think you'll like this' – Paddy Locke), and a couple of thrillers set in Australia. (There was an Aboriginal detective he found unbelievable. Still . . .)

175

Outside was a garden of sorts. He walked into dawn and looked at the drooping plants he'd struggled to establish in front of the stumps of his drooping house. There was never enough water in the tanks to sustain them through the dry. He'd managed to get a bush lemon growing and each spring – or what passed for spring – had planted beans and tomatoes that gave scabby fruitings. He nurtured vast images of sterility.

When he received the first notice of overdue rates, he'd ridden his bicycle into Red Plains and put his case to the uninterested girl working the inquiry desk in the council chambers.

'Don't get much for the rates,' he said. 'No water. No garbage removal, not even a decent road. The gravel's cut to pieces.'

'Sorry,' she'd said, not sorry. 'I'm just the clerk. You'd have to take it up with the councillors.' She tossed an impudent blonde mane.

What was the use?

The next time he was in town buying a few washers for his taps at Briceland's hardware store, he brought the matter up.

'It's like this, Benny,' Howard explained, leaning confidentially over the counter. (Did he know it was brother to brother?) 'The value of land's going up round here, see. That's what the rates are based on. We plan to run the town water pipes right out past yours and Mrs

176

Locke's place and that will bring the rates up even higher, eh? Council's starting on that next month. There's a new subdivision going up at the five mile.'

'Got two tanks. Won't need it.'

'You're lying, Benny,' Howie said jovially. 'You need all the water you can get out there. And even if you didn't connect, you'd still have to pay for the service. If it's there and you don't choose to hook up, that's your problem. You've still got to pay.'

The pipes had gone past in a nightmare of graders, trenchers and dust that coated his house inside and out with a plummy skin he could never quite remove and after a while didn't try to. A faded royal red.

Like the dusty geranium he now picked, rubbing the leaves between his fingers so he could carry that marvellous fragrance with him. The pipes had gone past and he didn't hook up and his rates rose and the payments soon got beyond him. It was as if the trenchers had dug him out with the clods of red earth and flung him to one side.

He sniffed once more at the crushed leaves. It was time to be going.

Ever since she'd settled in the house beyond his, gutsy Mrs Locke had always been friendly. Right from the start, he remembered, she'd pull up in her semi-ute as he pedalled his way into the township and say, 'Toss that mad contraption in the back, Benny. I'll give you a lift.'

Over the years they'd become friends in an undemanding way. She'd turn up at his door in the morning with a few pots of jam and ask if he needed a ride into town or if there was anything she could pick up for him. In return he would do odd jobs about her garden, fix guttering, patch up rotting timbers. There would be cups of tea afterwards and unprobing conversations that skittered around banalities of weather and town. When she got to know him a little better she would lend him books. She had a wall of them in her front room. Once she had begun talking about Chardin's notion of the Omega point, the ultimate integration of all individual consciousness.

'That's where evolution's heading, Benny.'

'You mean all of us, even no-good –'

She interrupted him before he could utter the words she knew were coming. 'All of us. The whole of humanity. All all all. Even a crusty old dame like me.'

Always she understood the delicacy, the fragility of the reclusiveness he had pulled around him like a cloak. From the few remarks Benny picked up while he drank his rare beer at the Lizard, he knew townsfolk thought she was a nutter. He didn't. She'd begun reading circles, drama and discussion groups, and tried to drag cake-baking homestead wives into university extension courses on ethics and contemporary religions. 'Give over,

Paddy,' they'd say. 'Get real. No one out here's got time for that sort of stuff.' Once in the Red Plains supermarket, driven crazy by the screeching of rock singers as she shopped, she had pretended to faint outside the manager's office and after he had helped her to a chair and raced off to fetch a female assistant, she had wedged the office door shut with a chock she had brought specially for that purpose and switched the hell tape in his machine for the first movement of the Sibelius second, of which she was particularly fond.

Despite the hammering on the door and the cries of outrage, she managed to keep the irate gent at bay for the entire movement, after which she removed the door-stop and opened up to his pulsing face, the blander smirk of the local sergeant and a crowd of paused and grinning shoppers. 'There,' she had said. 'Now, wasn't that lovely? Such a change for you all.'

She was charged and fined for creating a public nuisance and the blare of rock continued to yammer and shake the food aisles packed with goodies that had passed their use-by date.

She didn't give a hoot for the stories that budded in the telling and clambered about her mythic persona like scrub creeper. As a gesture she drank alone one night a week in the ladies' lounge at the Lizard, ignoring the scowls of male customers. She was making a statement. She was kindly, honest and her own woman.

She had heard about Benny Shoforth's imminent eviction and had marched in on him a fortnight before, offering help, suggesting he move to the old barn at the rear of her property. But Benny had become as independent as she.

'No,' he'd said. 'I've planned out what I'm going to do.'

'And what's that?'

He hesitated, fumbling with his cup, staring away from her across the verandah of her house to the flat plains in the west, the gidgee clumps lonely as himself.

'Listen, Benny,' she insisted, leaning forward in her chair and making him meet her eyes, 'whatever you've decided is fine by me. It won't go beyond, okay?'

'I've found a place.'

'Found?'

'Sort of. Out in the Isla Gorge.'

'What sort of place, Benny?'

He started to grin. 'First class, missus.'

'First-class what?'

'Well, there's this cave, bit of a rockpool, way off the beaten track. I could camp out there for a bit till I think out what I want to do.'

Paddy put her own cup down and found tears starting.

'Come here,' she said. 'Come and stay on my place for a while.'

'Can't do that, Paddy.' He didn't often use her first name. 'Like I said. Can't do that.'

She was blocked by his gentle smiling face. 'Then can I help you move? Can I run you out there? You can't take that lounge suite on your bike.'

He laughed, as she'd meant him to. 'Matter of fact,' he told her, 'I didn't want to leave that behind. It's all I've got to remind me of the family.'

'Heirloom stuff,' Paddy suggested, joking (that worn pile, those jabbing springs!), cutting the edge off the words with her hand just touching his arm. 'Don't worry. We'll take a run out this week.'

It was more than fifty kilometres to the granite hills and ravines that formed the park, a lonely road where the bitumen ended suddenly and became a tributary gravel stretch that soon became a track, then a line of wheel ruts made by lone bikers and the occasional park ranger. Rock humps loomed over them as the truck cut between spurs of the hill-line.

'Not far now,' he had said. 'About another half-mile.'

They pulled up on a sandy stretch above a creek that was more a chain of secret waterholes. Leaves dangled their still and pointed knives amid a shrilling of cicadas that only magnified that stillness until it swamped them sitting there in the truck. Overhead a wedgetailed eagle circled the gorge in a giant arc of air. Sky geometry. Nothing else moved.

Paddy climbed down and walked across to a dark unmoving circle of water. She shivered slightly in the hot midday. 'I don't like the feel,' she said. 'There's something wrong.'

Benny stood watching. He grunted then bent down and scooped a handful of creek-water and drank. It was sweet. Part black, part white, he understood that settler fright. Scrub. Scrub-scare! It was alien, spiky, unwelcoming. To them, anyway.

Reaching out he broke off a twig from a grey wattle. 'Here,' he said. 'Try this. Wood smells like violets. Nothing wrong with that.'

She held the twig to her nose and trapped the elusive scent. Then she smiled. 'Okay. I'm being stupid. Let's see what you've picked out for a camp-site.'

She followed him along the bank of the watercourse where it swung sharply in towards the cliffs, lurching into a thickness of tree that hid them from the track. A few metres back from the creek, boulders had dropped and formed a shallow cave whose sandy floor stretched down towards one of the waterholes.

'Here,' Benny said. 'This is it.'

'Here?' She stared unbelieving at the depression in the cliff face.

'Yes, here. It suits me fine. Came out a month ago and camped for a week.' He kicked the sand about on the cave floor and she saw ash traces of his fire.

'It's too far,' she said hopelessly. 'What if you're sick, Benny? It's miles from the nearest town. You've only got that damn crazy bike. You can't do this.'

He didn't want to argue. He was too old for fighting the system, too old to care about anything except the terminus. 'Just help me,' he said.

They went back to the truck and Paddy opened a thermos and poured out mugs of tea. Gobsmacked. What was there to say?

Early in the morning of the last day, Benny's last day in his home of ten years, Paddy Locke parked her truck in front of his verandah. His possessions were crammed in two cardboard boxes he had obtained from the supermarket in Red Plains. His clothes. His six books. Cooking utensils and tucker. His camp stretcher was neatly folded with bedding roped onto it.

'That's it?'

Benny grinned. 'Not quite.' He led her inside and nodded at the three-piecer his mother had owned and the small table and chairs. 'There's the heavy stuff.'

She looked at him and back at the lounge suite and

back at him and suddenly began to laugh. The thought of that housemaker's cliché squatting sedate in a cave in the middle of the scrub was a stunning irony.

'I like it!' she said. 'I like it!' and began laughing again till her laughter petered out in the puzzled hurt on Benny's face.

The three-seater weighed a ton. They dragged it out of his sitting-room and onto the verandah and then Paddy said she had to stop for a rest. They sat on it and stared at the paddocks across the road already marked out with surveyor's pegs.

'What time do you expect the terminators?'

Even at the pain-point of this moment Benny had to grin. It could be any time that day, he told her. But really he'd like to be gone before anyone came. He wanted to undercut the council's victory by his absence, not let them be spectators at his final humiliation. His whole body vibrated and rang with departures.

After a few moments they started work on the big settee again, managing to bump it down the steps and up to the tailboard of the truck. They stood panting and examined the situation.

'Jesus, Benny,' Paddy cried, 'we'll never do it.'

'I gotta do it,' he said. 'Gotta! Grab the far end.'

He was quickened by age-old affronts as he wedged himself under the top end of the settee and began raising himself, slowly, agonisingly, until he could edge the front legs over the truck rim. He could hear his heart drumming against the thin walls of his body as he eased himself out and went back to help Paddy shove the settee further onto the tray. One on each side they hoisted and thrust and the settee slid in a couple of feet and he said to her, 'You get back now and I'll do the rest,' and she said, 'Nonsense, Benny, I'm cursed by youth,' and for three minutes of muscle-rack tearing at their elderly backs they shoved until the lumpy thing was three-quarters on and they could pause.

'The rest's a breeze,' old Benny Shoforth said.

He went back to the house and trundled the single chairs out one at a time and between them they got them on top of the truck, packed in with the boxes, the bedding, the table. Then she followed him inside to check on anything forgotten. The sun stared at them both through the windows while the house sang a small wistful song of emptiness.

It took them half the morning to move the furniture from truck to cave.

They lugged the settee up the track by swinging one end forward, then the other, a kind of diagonal peg-legged walking, a process they could keep up for only a few minutes at a time.

Halfway there, Paddy Locke downed tools suddenly and produced the thermos and they sat on the lounge in the middle of scrub and sipped tea from plastic mugs. Benny could see how crazy they must look, two old codgers taking their work break on worn Genoa velvet with the sound of cicadas rubbing at the sky, scrubbing the air like sandpaper. The wedgetail soared back, swinging over the country where they sat enclosed, then rose on a thermal, taking in the world.

'That's how I'd like to be,' Benny said. 'Really like to be. Up there away from all this.'

'All this what?'

'All this trouble. The house. All of that.'

He looked down at his near-empty mug and tipped the last drops of tea onto the track. He'd taken pride in never being a troublemaker. He'd accepted and accepted with the passivity that was a natural part of the way of things since boyhood. It didn't make him feel any less a man. His dignity had remained intact. But now as he scuffed his worn shoes in the dirt and grass and looked at his few possessions scattered at intervals beneath the trees, he was aware of an alien chafe, that ancient anger against the way things were and the powerlessness of poverty and colour.

'There's still one box in the back of the truck,' Paddy said.

'That's yours.'

'No. It's yours. Let's finish getting old velvet up to the cave and then we can go back and fetch the small stuff.'

When things were finally arranged, the cave took on the quality of a macabre joke. Benny organised a cooking place just beneath the overhang of granite and stacked his skillet and bush kettle on a rough shelf made from a fence paling. At the back of the cave he set up his bunk and stacked his six books alongside like relics from a different world. He propped his bicycle up against one rocky wall.

'This is crazy,' Paddy said. ' You know you're always welcome.'

'I know.' Benny nodded. He spotted tears in the woman's eyes and didn't want any fuss.

'You've forgotten that last box!' she reminded him.

Benny walked back to the truck and brought it over to Paddy who was sitting on the settee staring down across the strip of sand towards the small waterhole.

'Just a few things you might need,' she said, watching as he pulled back the cardboard flaps. There were tins of beans, soup, powdered milk, jars of honey and sugar, a couple of packets of tea.

'Can't take this,' he protested. 'Not all this.'

'It's not much,' she said. 'House-warming present. Here's happy days, Benny!'

'Yair.' He looked at her and away. 'Happy days.'

And then they both tried to chuckle, neither of them sure at what.

'I'll be checking on you,' she mock warned. 'I'll be out to see how you're going.' He looked so small, so frail. His face was creased in lines of fatigue.

She slapped one of the cushions as she rose. 'Autumn tonings indeed!'

She kept her word. Within the fortnight she drove out again to see how Benny was getting on. He was sitting over a small campfire by the waterhole, a billy bubbling ready for him to drop the tea leaves in. He looked thinner, said less. No, he insisted, he was happy. He was managing fine. She unloaded some bread she had baked especially and a small sack of potatoes and pumpkin.

'It's too much,' he protested. 'You can't keep doing this.'

'I'm fine. I've a bit put by.' She was hating what they had done to him.

The council man sent along to take possession of Benny's property had been curious and pestered with questions. They were like some irritating rash. 'Where's he gone?' he demanded. 'Must have gone some place.'

She had pleaded ignorance. Two council functionaries returned a week later. Why should they care? Their persistence hardened her resolve. Benny Shoforth had been seen riding his bicycle into Red Plains to pick up his

pension cheque and the few things he needed. Howie
Briceland had buttonholed him outside the supermarket
and probed but Benny stayed calm, unresponsive to
questioning. Every time he looked at Briceland these
days he wanted to accuse, 'You're my half-brother. We've
got the same dad.' He wanted to shatter that confidence,
that master-race assurance.

But he didn't. He looked at Briceland's smoothly
shaven face with its ginger sprout of eyebrows above the
reddened blue gaze and saw the bone structure that
twinned his own. 'I'm coping,' he said. And wouldn't say
more.

One day a month or so after Benny had moved to the
gorge, Briceland became a spy, eaten up to discover. Mrs
Locke had just purchased extra kerosene and a small
primus. No questions fazed her. She was too glib. He
knew she knew.

Leaving his assistant in charge of the store, he slipped
out the back to his car and followed her truck, now a
mile-distant speck almost obscured by dust-murk, until
he saw it swing off the main road and head out on the
branch towards the gorge. Whistling, he drove past the
turn-off and into Red Plains where he had a celebratory
beer. 'Snap!' he said aloud to no one at all.

Hunting gave purpose.

On the next pension day he drove into Red Plains and
gossiped with the shire clerk in front of the council

chambers until he caught sight of Benny Shoforth pedalling his crazy bicycle along the shopping strip. Abruptly he stubbed out his cigarette, croaked matey farewells, and unable to understand this bubbling joy within drove out of town to the gorge road. It didn't take him long to find Benny's camp-site.

'Jesus!' Howie Briceland said to a bunch of his drinking mates that night at the Lizard. 'You wouldn't believe it! A fucking three-piece lounge suite stuck up in a cave above the creek. Imagine!'

They all imagined and responded with the quacks of laughter Howie Briceland expected.

'Well, it's not on! He can't stay. My God, it's national park. Let one in and we'll have a mob of ferals stuck all over the place with their tin humpies and plantations of pot!'

'He's a bit of a boong, isn't he?' one of the men commented. 'Hard to tell, though. Still, he could live off the land better than most.'

Howie Briceland bit his lip. He wasn't too sure about letting this side issue dominate. There'd been stories about his old man he'd overheard when he was a kid. Taking that line, he suspected, would open sore places. Establishment ground would tremble beneath him.

'No, mate. That's not what's important.' He groped round for buzz words. 'It's the ecology we've got to think about. And tourism. Carnarvon Gorge packs in thousands of visitors a year. I think we should start getting our own place moving. Bring the district alive.'

There were half-hearted beery assents. Howie was not popular. He was feared. He had money, a native arrogance, and was on fawning terms with a number of politicians. But envy – and he knew this – was always nibbling at the perimeters of success and even as he shouted the next round he could sense a dislike of patronage along with the taking. The eager glass-grasping hands made him smile sourly.

He let the matter drop, deciding there was more available help in Red Plains. A clearance! A purge! He'd never liked Benny Shoforth, never understood that quiet reserve, the tempered replies to overtures in store or pub. He liked to know what a feller was thinking. The loud bugger, his old man had lectured him (uselessly), is the exposed bugger.

The itch persisted.

He drove out to the gorge late one afternoon and confronted Benny Shoforth who was dangling a peaceful line in the pool. 'You've got to move,' he told him. He told him that the park hadn't been gazetted for campers. He told him he was creating health and fire risks.

'No,' Benny said.

'You deaf, mate? I said you got to go!'

'No,' Benny said.

The story got around. Drinking buddies nudged each other when they saw Howie Briceland coming.

Briceland loathed being the town joke. What he said went! He was being made to look a fool.

Impatiently he waited a few days before he finally succumbed and rang the Department of Parks and Wildlife Services. 'Wildlife!' he muttered as he waited on the telephone's end. They kept playing some god-awful classical stuff while he hung there like a trapped fly. He persuaded one of the rangers to go out and inspect. 'Tell him he's got to move!' he ordered.

The ranger reported back by the end of the week. Mr Shoforth, he told nail-biting Howie Briceland, refused to leave.

'We'll see about that,' Briceland snarled before hanging up.

Another week.

He enlisted the aid of the Red Plains police sergeant. He explained the situation in exaggerated detail. He hinted at political intervention for a city transfer.

'She'll be right,' the sergeant assured him. 'No worries.'

The sergeant, followed by the ranger in his truck, drove out to the gorge and threatened Benny with arrest. 'This stuff!' the sergeant said contemptuously, waving a hand at the lounge suite and bed. 'This stuff has got to go, see. You're creating a fire hazard out here.'

'No,' Benny said.

'Sorry, mate,' the sergeant said, 'but that's the way it is. We're taking you and the rest of your things back into town. No argument.'

Benny stood quietly watching as the ranger and sergeant humped his belongings along the track and heaved them onto the ranger's truck. They were panting and angry by the time they finished and the sergeant, glaring at Benny, ordered him into the patrol car.

It was when they tried to turn out of the track that they found their way blocked by Paddy Locke's utility angled across the ruts. Forewarned by a sly something in Briceland's eye the last time they had spoken, she had driven out early for her fortnightly check on Benny.

Pension day. All the dinosaurs in town buying their mince steak and bread, their pathetic tins of canned food.

'Where's old Benny?' Briceland had asked her. Testing. 'You know where he is, don't you?'

She had looked at him coolly. 'Why should I know?'

'Had an idea you were mates. Well, lady, you're not the only one with secrets.'

'Why can't you drop it?' she said. 'You got what you wanted. You forced him out of his home. Isn't that enough?' She stumped away and went into the newsagency.

Now she stood in front of the men, intractable, glaring at the furniture piled on the ranger's truck. She lied ferociously. 'That's my stuff you've got there,' she snapped. 'I lent it to Benny. You can put it straight back onto my truck and I'll take it home. Benny's coming with me for a while till I find him a place somewhere else.'

They didn't believe her.

'Now!' she shouted. 'Now!'

Benny was restless in Paddy's back verandah sleepout. Each day the silence he carried within deepened. Something will turn up, Paddy kept assuring him. Something.

He would nod and amble out to the garden and work till the midday heat drove him back to sit in the shade of the awnings.

Towards the end of his second week with her, Paddy announced that she was driving into Red Plains that evening for a council meeting that was open to the locals for public comment on the new development.

'I think I'll come,' Benny said. His desire for payback surprised him.

The council chambers were filled that night with Red Plains dwellers who resented the water pipes running out of Drylands when the town badly needed a swimming-pool. There was a sprinkling of Drylands graziers, the local member, and an advisory engineer who had come in from the coast.

Benny sat next to Paddy near the front of the room

where he could watch the seated councillors as they dealt with various matters before public discussion began. He could not take his eyes from Howie Briceland who had abandoned his man-of-the-people gear and sported a sharp two-piecer and jazzy tie.

The moment the meeting was thrown open, Benny rose and pushed his way past Paddy to the aisle. He ignored yells telling him to sit. He strode down until he was facing the councillors where they sat, smug, he thought, he hated, at the long table. But he could see only Howie Briceland. Behind Benny the packed seats rustled with interest.

'Why?' Benny demanded, voice raised, looking directly at Briceland. 'Why did you do that to me?'

'I don't know what you're talking about, mate,' Briceland said. He whispered to the man next to him, 'Get someone to get that bastard out of here.'

'Why?' Benny cried loudly. 'I'm your brother.'

The room was stilled.

Benny stepped into shadow as he drew close to the table. 'Same father,' the shadowed man called, again loudly and clearly, moving nearer until his face thrust its tired bones towards Briceland, so dangerously threateningly intimate the other man leant back in his chair. 'Your half-brother.'

'Bullshit!' Briceland yelled, pressing down the truth he had known for years. 'Bloody prove it!'

The breaths of both men were audible rasps in the shocked air. Already the councillors were nudging, grinning. There were sniggers from the audience.

It was one no-count man's word against his, Briceland thought confusedly. But the lingering stink of accusation? Public censure? Would there be that? There were weather changes, these days, in popular attitudes. Mentally his mind bluffed around with words like 'national park', 'public interest', 'trespass'. Their implied excuse rang like a dud coin even he could hear. He rose and leaned across the table blathering meaninglessly.

A slow clapping began.

Watching, Paddy stiffened as she saw two self-appointed bouncers run across from the side. Her stomach clenched. Her hands began to shake. Other people around her began standing, shoving to reach whatever mêlée might occur, their faces lit with anticipatory malice.

Arms wound about Benny Shoforth's shoulders. Hands dragged his slight body back from the table. The ancient resentments rose in his mouth like bile before he could discover obliteration.

He turned his face to the buzzing crowd now moving in and shouted into the night, 'I'm Kanolu tribe, you hear? His brother! His brother! Kanolu! Kanolu!'

The words wouldn't stop vomiting from his mouth.

MEANWHILE . . .

If she could open up one word only and watch it expand from bud to fully formed calyx, sepals, corolla, biologically perfect, would she be satisfied with that?

A word could have a whole fiction buried within. One word, monosyllabic or polysyllabic – take your pick – opened up a worldscape of ideas that could laze in bliss under summer soothings or become a maelstrom of conflict.

Tap and tap.

She thought this, she thought about the shadows of the shadows of words – hopeless! – and slammed the cover back on her typewriter, overcome by the illusion of what she was doing. Was illusion the wrong word? The difficulty, perhaps.

Six o'clock. The burnt-out ends of. She had closed the

shop and gone upstairs for a cup of tea. Through her window looking down on the main street she could see the cars and trucks moving in to park outside the pub. Clem had recently installed a satellite dish and linked up to a sports channel. It was, Janet thought, a symbol of male religion: there they all were, yappings stilled as they attended League mass, quaffing their communion Tooheys, joining in the votive prayers of groan, chiack, cheer.

Beaudy, Clem!

As she watched, sipping her tea, hearing the television boom through the open verandah doors of the Legless Lizard, someone who had just parked a little way beyond the pub looked up and saw her watching. A hand waved. She waved back. Then she saw the waving hand give her the finger.

Quickly she drew back, slopping tea and confusion, sprung as some sort of nosey-bob spy. Indignant. Angry. Embarrassed.

She remembered the disturbance on her desk, the merest of flutter-probe that alerted her to the fact that she was being discussed, talked about. Lately there had been the stray question cloaked in sympathetic interest: 'Janet, wotcher do in the evening, love? Must get lonely, eh?'

There was that one night two weeks ago when she had yielded to an invitation from Paddy Locke and trotted across for a shandy in the ladies' lounge. The noise inside had cracked her head apart. Conversation was impossible. Clem winked at her sympathetically when he brought in their drinks and managed to howl in her ear, 'Have to do it. It's part of the ambience!'

Ambience! Shambience!

It was the shire clerk who had given her the finger, a sallow streak of a man who had come back freaked out by the Vietnam War, married a cheerful personnel girl from a commercial radio station and efficiently immobilised her by siring six sons in as many years. He used phrases like 'the lady wife' and 'the little woman' and believed in football codes as if they were the Mosaic Law. Clem's sports channel drew him nightly to the Lizard like a magnet.

This street. This town. The four shops.

Her business wasn't doing well, hadn't been doing well for the last three years. Own up! It was dying. Newspapers, trinkets and toys for the kids at Christmas, the occasional greeting card. Her stock of stationery had lowered barely an inch in two years. No one wrote. No one read except Paddy Locke. Even the westerns and thrillers had turned yellow on the racks. Their foxing became hers. Sighing, she looked at her hands and inspected the mildew of time.

She was beginning to think that some corrupt and deliberate policy was behind the system that produced school leavers and even university graduates barely literate in their own tongue. Was there a plot to take the whole economy back five hundred years to a kind of feudalism in which the minority wealthy had control of a population that was employable only for the most menial of occupations and would be grateful for pittances, serf-style?

She poured herself a fresh cup of tea and went back to the front window. The television boom was rockfall, avalanche, erratic billow. While she watched a lilac dusk settle on the street and lights pick out their half-mile of council concern, she saw the small runabout of Mrs Shire Clerk pull in and the shire clerk's wife, followed by her two chunky youngest, now twelve and thirteen, poke her head dispiritedly around the bar-room door. In the sudden blaze of light, with her dragging kids, she had less the appearance of a fury than a wretched mendicant come to plead the case for an over-warmed dinner-wilting, a beggar wanting to get done the last chores of the day.

All the way to Canossa, Janet murmured. Practically on her knees!

The shire clerk's wife reappeared, a kid each side of her narrow body, and behind, chivvying, her husband in full verbal spate, hurling words as she almost ran back to the car and hustled the boys in. Under the streetlight her face was distorted by – chagrin? tears? humiliation? rage?

Janet finished her tea and returned to the table where

her typewriter stood and began dispelling loneliness with the sound of keys clacking over visitants who were not and yet were at the same time wholly within these dingy walls.

Pull out, Ted advised as she typed away. Pull out while you still have the energy.

'I can't,' she whispered aloud. 'Not yet. Something ties me to this place. Anyway, nothing's selling. Where would the money come from, even if I wanted to make the break?'

Leave it, Ted's voice kept urging. Leave leave leave.

His voice became the leaf sound on the back wall, the cockroach scuttle under the sink, the silence of silverfish along the shelves.

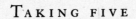
TAKING FIVE

It was as Lannie Cunneen was fixing her nine thousand, three hundred and twenty-eighth school lunch that she suddenly downed tools and scribbled on the kitchen notepad *I can't do this any more. I can't bear it* and went out to her small car and drove off, still in her dressing-gown and slippers.

She drove all morning and well into the afternoon until she brought herself and the car to a stop on a small knoll overlooking Emu Park beach. Bemused, she sat there staring at blue water. She was beyond thought and had merely a sense of catharsis and, after that, of escape. Bliss! She didn't even feel the pangs of hunger. It was only towards five o'clock that thirst overtook her and she realised she had gone off without her purse. She rooted around in the glovebox and found a few dollars in small change under a tangle of supermarket dockets. She blinked and turned her eyes away from the mesmeric sea, put the car into gear and drove along the front to a shop.

It was full of kids buying icecream and milkshakes. They all stared, nudged and sniggered. She had forgotten the dressing-gown. 'Versace,' she said. 'The latest. A glass of milk, please.'

The shoplady served her while her husband went to the phone to report a nutter. Then she took her milk in its plastic tumbler out to the car, drank it and drove back to the headland where, deliciously freed, oblivious almost to any nagging concerns about what lay behind, she fell asleep lulled by the steady rhythm of water breaking on the sand below.

Two hours later she was woken by torch-dance jazzing through the windscreen and a blue-uniformed man beating his hand on the locked door. Obligingly she flicked the lock and opened it, dazzled by flashlight and wondering for a moment where she was.

'Yes?' she asked.

'You okay, lady?' the policeman said. His offsider was standing back near the police car, its blue lights pulsating, its engine throbbing.

Lannie found she couldn't answer. She simply gaped.

'Your husband got in touch,' the copper went on. 'He's been worried sick. You'd better come back with us to the station. He's driving down to fetch you.'

Still no words came. She decided suddenly that it was

208

better not to speak. She leaned back in her seat, her hands clutching the worn edges.

'All right now, lady. Step on out and we'll lock the car up and everything will be okay.'

But it wouldn't. Nothing was okay. She gripped the edges of her seat more tightly.

'Look!' The copper was becoming impatient. 'You've gotta step out, right? Otherwise I'll have to arrest you.'

She heard herself mutter, 'Seven thousand, three hundred approximately.'

'What's that? What's that you're saying?'

'Three thousand and twenty.'

'Lissen, lady, I don't know what the hell you're talking about. Come on now, hop out. I don't want to have to use force.'

'Nine thousand, three hundred and twenty-eight. There were two more to go.'

The copper leant forward, put muscular arms about her shoulders and half lifted, half dragged Lannie Cunneen from the driving seat. She stood in the colder night air from the sea, shivering in her dressing-gown but remaining dignified.

'Car keys,' the copper demanded.

She handed them over in silence and he kicked the door shut and locked it. He couldn't cope with this stuff. His offsider was trying not to laugh. Lannie closed her eyes as they frogmarched her to the police car and drove back to the station where someone organised a chair, a cup of tea, and left her sitting alone in an interview room.

She dozed, walked, sat, dozed. There was a permanent pain up the back of her neck and between her shoulders. She thought of nothing.

At about four in the morning they brought her husband in, angry and exhausted from an all-night drive. His eyes were puffed and there was a large smear of oil down one cheek.

'Now, what's all this about?' he asked irritably. 'Jesus, Lannie, have you led me a dance!'

He smiled, a part-smile, somehow bitter, somehow unplacating. Halfway across the room it dropped to the lino tiles.

'We have to go back. Now.'

She looked up at him. She couldn't, wouldn't drive. Not back. Perhaps she could be taken, but she was not going voluntarily. Attempting a soother, he would get someone to pick up her car, he told her. Then, half pushing, half dragging, he got her back to his own car parked outside. The town wore the expectant stippled grey of pre-dawn, as if maybe this one, this now-morrow, could hold answers. It wouldn't.

The duty sergeant stood on the lighted verandah of the police station and watched them leave. He didn't know which one to feel sorrier for.

'Why?' her husband asked. She said nothing.

He drove grimly, exhausted, furious, his back to the sunrise, scooping mile after mile from the distance between here and there. She leaned against the passenger window and slept in broken passages of numbness. Occasionally when she woke and shifted her head into a more comfortable position he said, 'Why?' but she hardly heard the monosyllable and couldn't have given a reason. She gave him numbers. In thousands.

'Look at me,' she said to the pudgy psychiatrist in a dreary room of medical offices in Rockhampton, 'nudging forty, married for twenty years, six boys, all at school, and an endless...' Her silence lengthened and coiled about the whole room, the appalling landscapes done by local artists, the fake leather couch she had refused to use, the important desk.

'Yes?' the psychiatrist prodded.

'After twenty years you hardly know what sex you are.'

The psychiatrist brightened at this. He was balding, had the beginnings of a luncheon gut, and an all-consuming weariness with the endless petty problems of neurotics. He had also, one patient had told him with annoyance, the habit of glancing at his watch halfway through each session, with even more furtive timekeepings as the expensive half-hour neared its end. He kept his eyes on the woman opposite and waited. Unfortunately she didn't appear anxious to fill the terrible gaps.

He glanced at his notes. 'Your husband tells me you keep mentioning numbers. Um, why is that?'

She looked at him. 'Are you married?'

'Yes.'

'Do you have children?'

'Three.' He rather resented this but thought he had better humour her.

'Have you ever had sole care of them for, say, even a week? Have you?'

'Is that relevant?'

'Have you?'

'No, I must admit. But –'

'I have six,' she said, ' all school age. I have made rough estimates of the numbers of dinners, breakfasts, lunches, washings and ironings over twenty years of bliss.'

The psychiatrist was irritated by her ironic tone. Another of these feminist whingers!

'But surely the boys give a hand?'

'My husband won't allow it. He says it's women's work. He believes a woman's place is in the home. Permanently. He's keen for the boys to be footballers and drinkers. That's manly.' She paused. 'Three hundred and sixty,' she said.

'I beg your pardon?'

'I'm just totting up the number of football shorts and jerseys I wash and iron in a season.'

The psychiatrist allowed himself a small smile.

'But other interests? Surely there are women's groups, club activities, holidays?'

'Holidays!' She gave a grimace. 'One.'

It was terrible and funny at the same time to remember.

She supposed it was a honeymoon.

Whirlwind was the spurious word applied to rapid courtships. Well, yes. A fortnight of dates with this lanky veteran who had been a volunteer rather than conscript for the Vietnam massacres. That should have told her something!

They had met on the deck of a launch going over to Stradbroke and perhaps the salt of bay air, perhaps the whipped-cream quality of bay waves reduced her usually acute perceptions. He had interrupted a law course to enlist, he told her. He believed in the domino theory and the threat of communism. She responded with a description of her work at a commercial radio station, researching for mouth-jocks on a teenage pop programme. She wasn't crazy about it but hoped for advancement to something better. He had laughed in a generous and understanding way. They met again. And again. He was tinkering with the idea of giving up law and trying for a position in local government. His background, he said solemnly, should give him an edge.

Vietnam had spoiled him for study. He wanted a job, an income, a *settled* background.

Bingo! she realised now. She was to be that. She was careless about the ripple effect of words. How could she not be at twenty and working on popular radio where the depth of analysis plummeted in direct ratio to the high-pitched screech of commentator indignation.

They married within the month.

'I don't want my wife working,' he announced with memories of female Asian compliance.

She gave up her job. They went on a honeymoon to India.

India! she had marvelled. Another country and culture! She grabbed brochures, borrowed books, gawped at deliciously coloured and thoughtfully edited photographs of the subcontinent. Only Fred would think of something so exotic.

Why India? Was he missing the East?

They stayed for three nights at a two-star hotel in Bombay where they walked almost everywhere. They ate at street stalls. She suspected him of stinginess, a suspicion underlined when he suggested they see the country by staying at backpacker hostels for the next fortnight. They had already moved into one that was stunningly uncomfortable, grimy and overcrowded with hippies and would-be gurus in search of nirvana.

Why?

'I want to go home,' she whimpered, stupefied by heat and stomach upset. 'Please, Fred.'

'Nonsense!' He gave her a little hug. 'What's happened to that keen adventurer eager for new experiences I met back in Brisbane? Where's she gone?'

He told her he knew members of a small commune of Australians living on the beach near Goa. They would bus or train or hitch.

Was this why?

He told her this while they were trudging along Victoria Road on their way to the gardens. Not far from the gates there was a beggar, legless, blind, bundled over his tray, arms flapping into the thick air as he begged for alms.

'Please?' she had beseeched Fred. 'Please give him something.' Fred was in charge of all the funds.

'I can't get at my wallet,' he said testily. 'It's in my money belt.' He groped in one pocket after another and came up with a handful of boiled sweets. 'There,' he said heartily, dropping them on the tray beside the few coins already there. 'Enjoy.'

She had seen the sweets were still wrapped in paper. 'He's blind. He won't be able to unwrap them.'

'Oh,' Fred had said, pausing, considering. Then he bent down to take them back and there was a frightful scene as the blind man dropped forward to protect his wealth, his arms wrestling with Fred's as they tussled for the lollies. There were disgusting grunting sounds. In no time a crowd had gathered and she walked away, away from the gardens and back towards the dingy back-packers, into the screech of car horns, the clogged gasoline-filled air, the thrusting crowds.

Fred caught up with her a block farther on. He was red with indignation. A policeman had questioned him and moved him on.

For hours Lannie felt she couldn't speak to him, and they never did attempt heading down the coast but had wilted away in a fortnight of armed truce. And anyway, when the time came to board the plane, she suspected she was pregnant.

This is the way it goes, she told herself. This is the way.

Nineteen years on a property sixteen kilometres out of Red Plains and Drylands, the apex of a triangle created by gravel roads and spinifex whose hypotenuse led directly to the Legless Lizard. Legless lizards have rudimentary limbs. Well, *that's* about right, she decided with a wry smile. A dried-out creek and dams little more than quagmires, a few sheep that Fred kept totter-ing around as a tax lurk and six bouncing boys – the eldest was repeating final year high school – whose sole interest was football.

For most of those nineteen years Fred had worked in a clerical position at the Red Plains council chambers, allowing the farm to fall apart while he strove for promotion and eventually the position of shire clerk.

Goal!

The psychiatrist – Dr Kyle – ran a small and expensive therapy clinic as an adjunct to a private hospital. He had few takers. Most of the nutters roamed harmlessly about the streets of coastal towns or languished in places so far inland locals learned to live with them, underscoring the legend of idiosyncrasy monopolised by the north. But he managed to persuade Fred that his wife needed a month of treatment. 'And then we'll see how things are,' he added, smiling. 'Rest. Medication. A complete change of scene. But rest above all.'

'How will I cope?'

'Have you thought of employing a housekeeper? Surely the boys are old enough now to look after themselves. Why your youngest is – let me see – eleven? Twelve?'

Fred grunted. The cost was getting to him. Lannie sat indifferent in her chair, one foot tapping the packed bag her husband had brought in. Fred kissed her goodbye and the kiss, like his earlier smile, also dropped to the floor and fragmented.

She enjoyed the rest. She enjoyed having meals brought on trays. She read sometimes but mostly sat in the small courtyard of the clinic and stared into space. Every week Fred came to visit and to urge her back home but she was revelling in that very intermission Fred had allocated himself during the breakfast frenzy each morning. ('Fred, for Chrissake can you watch the toast while I do the eggs?' 'Sorry, love, I'm having my quiet time.')

He had trouble finding a housekeeper.

He had advertised the job as live-in, two hundred a week, all found. The first applicant who had gone out to the farm summed up the workload in minutes. 'Are you mad?' she said, and left. Grudgingly he raised the salary offered and persuaded an elderly widowed pensioner. She lasted a week.

'You'll have to come back, Lannie,' Fred said on his next weekend visit. 'We just can't cope.'

'A clinic is a lovesome thing, God wot!' Lannie said.

'What? What's that?'

'Never mind. I'm not coming back.'

'Stop your nonsense, love,' Fred said. He got up from the one easychair and walked about the small room painted depression blue. Outside on the tiny lawn an elderly woman was walking up and down talking to herself. She appeared to be amused by what she was saying and every now and again gave a chuckle. She waved happily to Fred's nosey face looking through the window and vanished into a side door.

'Let's go outside and talk this thing over,' Fred suggested.

'Must we?'

'Yes. Come on now. It's nicer outside.'

The heat was stunning. It hugged them in great clammy arms. Overhead clouds boiled up in giant clots that presaged the Wet, threatened and then rolled on out to sea while the sun struck again with venom. Fred led his wife to a table and chairs set under a mango tree. They were barely seated when an old man leaning heavily on a stick tottered out from the clinic and over to them.

'That's Mr Hartigan,' Lannie said. 'Hello, Mr Hartigan!'

Mr Hartigan smiled, a sad wisp of a smile that slid about his lips as if unsure of direction. He came closer to Lannie, removed his teeth and placed them gently on her lap like an offering. Then he fluttered a hand at her and limped away across the grass.

'Jesus God!' Fred cried. 'I'm taking you out of here. Look. You've had a rest. It's time you came home.'

'Sixty,' Lannie said. She stared straight past him.

'Sixty? What do you mean, bloody sixty?'

'The lunches I haven't had to cut for the last fortnight.'

'Oh God!' Fred said. He dropped his head in his hands.

'Would you like to talk to Father O'Shea? It couldn't be more unproductive than what's happening here.'

'Yes it could.'

Fred ignored the remark. 'And anyway, what's that with the teeth?'

'Poor old boy,' Lannie said. 'He gives them to everyone.' She folded the dentures into a hanky.

'Why, for God's sake?'

'They don't fucken fit. That's why! He kept leaving them on the reception desk at his dentist's and the dentist had him committed. Harassment, the dentist said. Fair world, isn't it?'

She looked past Fred and waved to the old lady, who had come outside once more and was sidling up to them. 'Hello, Mrs B,' Lannie said. 'Come over here and meet my husband.'

'I don't like husbands, dear,' the old lady said. She spun suddenly and turned away.

'Pack your bag,' Fred ordered, standing up, hands clenched in irritation, 'and I'll see Dr Kyle about checking you out of this place.'

'No. I'm starting to like it here.'

'What the hell do you want?' Fred's voice rose in the steamy heat of the small garden and his words hung above them like nimbus.

'I want a job.'

'You've got a job. Looking after your family.'

'Not that sort of job. A change of job. A change of direction. You know, Fred, you sound just like Father O'Shea! Look, I've spent twenty years of my life cooking washing ironing cleaning and I want something else. You don't understand, do you? The boys are quite old enough to cut their own lunches, wash their own daggy football shorts, help get meals. I'm sick to death of your telling them that's women's work. You make that simple fallacy all men make – you're physically more powerful, therefore you have total power and because you have total power you assume you are more intelligent! That's your mistake, jumping from muscles to brains. A mistake or cunning. So you proceed to shove and bully and treat wives like peasants. Well, this wife anyway. I'm sick to death of doing nothing but clean up after you all. I don't want more babies. I want a job that pays me something. I don't want to talk to that old fool O'Shea who's barely heard of Vatican II and who believes women should breed till they drop.' She bunged on a brogue. '"The hosband has roights, me dear."'

She glared at Fred. 'And what's more, the old bugger has a housekeeper to cook his chops. He understands nothing. Why don't you go, Fred, and leave me be.'

Fred's fingers curled and uncurled. He could hardly drag her, chair and all, out to the car. Someone might be watching.

'You *are* mad,' he said. 'The things you're saying.

Bloody mad. One more week.' His anger was a giant lump in his throat. 'One. I'll be over next Sunday evening.'

On the Friday morning very early before the rattle of teacups, Lannie packed her bag and left the clinic without seeing the matron, any of the day nurses or silky Dr Kyle. She booked herself into a bloodhouse hotel in town and set about job seeking. The heat might have squeezed out hope as she stepped along the Tropic that cut the town in half.

Twenty years out of the workforce. It was impossible, she judged, but she persisted. She approached the local radio station and after thirty minutes achieved an interview with the personnel manager who was having a boring day anyway and listened with half an ear as she outlined her background in commercial broadcasting.

'You weren't in it long,' he said. He looked at her critically. 'This isn't a good time to be job hunting. Everyone wants to be a radio jock.'

'I don't,' she said. She would push through layers of indifference. 'I'll do anything. Make tea, clear up back clerical work, answer telephones, organise appointments, do research. I can handle a computer. And I'll do it for a junior wage.'

222

'We can't do that,' he said. But his eyes brightened. 'General dogsbody, is that what you want?'

'That's what I want,' she lied, crossing fingers on her lap. Better things would come. She felt it in her bones.

He looked at her. He saw a slender, not young not old woman, neatly dressed, speaking confidently. He wouldn't mind a dash of efficiency about the place. And she appeared malleable. Malleability was all! The latest front-office appointee could barely read, forgot to take down messages and, when she did, her sub-literacy caused terrible problems with days of the week and appointment times. She spent hours on the phone talking to her boyfriend.

'We'll be in touch,' he said.

Four other firms said they'd be in touch. She was on the point of despairing decision. She would have to return to the farm. She missed the boys. She loved them. But she craved mobility, another identity than that of slave.

She took herself and what she felt was a wasted morning into a small coffee shop near the river and sipped moodily at her tea under a moodily turning fan. Flies buzzed and hurtled to death against the purple circle of light above the counter bar. She watched them. *Me*, she thought. *Me*.

She remembered Fred's first two visits to the clinic. He had brought the kids with him, the eldest driving half of them in her little runabout. They were curious and embarrassed. They had been bored. They had asked her to come back. She had said, 'I will if you'll help me.' And Fred had said, 'Now, now, Lannie, you know I won't have the boys turned into housewives.' The youngest, who was nearly twelve and already taller than his mother, had begged his father to let them go look round the town and find a hamburger and a video arcade. When they had gone Fred said, 'You can see how they miss you.'

'Not really,' she replied, watching her husband's eyes shift.

'Don't you love them?'

'Of course I love them.'

'Then why don't you come home?'

'I don't think they love me. They just miss what I do for them. I want a life. Just a bit of a life outside kitchen and the wash-house.'

'Not much wash-house.' It was a grim piece of jocularity. 'The tanks are just about empty.'

Peeved Lannie lost it. She began to yell.

'Then you'd want me to go down to the creekhole and beat the bloody clothes on rocks while I utter little orgastic cries of pleasure and the other wives look on and say, I want to do what she's doing?'

'Jesus, you're disgusting!' Fred said. 'Bloody disgusting. You're not being like the other wives now. They don't make unreasonable demands.'

224

'You're the problem,' she told him.

But he couldn't see it.

'Okay,' the personnel manager at the radio station said when she went back there on Monday after three days of silence. 'You can start tomorrow.' That morning he had been forced to sack the girl on the front desk when he surprised her making a lengthy overseas call to Los Angeles where her boyfriend was taking time off to find himself. Baby-doll sumptuousness wasn't worth it, he decided.

'I can start right now,' Lannie said, full of zeal.

Through the window she could see the busy streets of the town, slow-moving shoppers, cars cruising, cars angled in to the kerb. There was a glimpse of sluggish green-brown river and a man in a rowing boat pulling across to the north shore. She thought for a moment she recognised the stoop, the white thatch of hair.

Blink! Drylands! Blink!

'Fine,' the personnel manager was saying. 'Come out front and I'll give you a run-through. Can you handle a switchboard?'

'I'm a quick learner,' she assured him.

And she was.

That night she rang Fred from a pay phone at the post

office to tell him she'd be back at the weekend. But when he said, 'Where the hell have you been?' she hung up.

They had to talk this through.

She caught a bus back to Drylands late on Friday and hitched a lift out to the farm with Paddy Locke. Strangely enough, the house was not nearly as chaotic as she had expected, though Fred sulked and was inclined to whine. He had spent a fortune at the laundrette in Red Plains and another small fortune in bribing the boys to organise evening meals. The kitchen was a mess of striving.

'I'm not giving up this job,' she told him. 'But I'll be back each weekend to see how you and the boys are getting on. I need my car.'

Fred was appalled by a new businesslike quality in his wife's manner. He had been cramming his six sons into the panel van and running them in to Red Plains High each school day. He couldn't wait for the holidays a fortnight off. The afternoons were the worst, he explained almost tearfully to his wife, who sat and smiled and watched him. He had the choice, he said, of letting them hang round the town until he finished work at the council chambers or having them get the bus back to Drylands and wait about there. He'd tried organising a lift for them out to the farm each afternoon, but no one was willing to make it a regular chore. And the endless sports practices after school! His wife had timetabled her life around those. He felt he was going crazy. 'I need you, Lannie,' he half whimpered and surprisingly burst into tears.

She let him sob for a little. She felt it might calm him and perhaps they could discuss the whole thing rationally.

There was no discussion.

Tears weren't enough.

Fred had had her runabout driven back soon after she was admitted to the clinic. Now she drove its friendly clutter to the coast late on Sunday, having left the family two enormous casseroles and a batch of biscuits she had whipped up that morning. The boys had seemed indifferent to her presence but livened considerably when she explained she intended renting a house when things got established and that they could drive over on sport-free weekends and stay with her. Johnnie, the eldest, now had his licence and perhaps Dad would lend him the van. 'Cool,' they said at the thought of hanging out in the milk bars, malls, video arcades. And, 'See you!' they cried without a tear. 'See you!' Chappie, the youngest, was banging a basketball about and forgot to wave.

It was Lannie who drove back unable to see the road properly through her own grief. 'I was an automaton nothing,' she whispered. A nothing. Just something that supplied and supplied for the scrappiest of thanks, if ever. Even the rare holidays when Fred had rented the cheapest possible house at the beach had been a replay of the action back in Drylands.

'Makes a change, doesn't it?' Fred would cry proudly, surveying the narrow bedrooms with their stained mattresses, the kitchen with the blocked sink and the stove whose oven didn't work, the rusting fridge, the broken vacuum cleaner.

For a fortnight she cooked washed cleaned while the seven chaps headed off to surf fish sunbake, leaving her wrestling with idiosyncratic stove and washing machine, and returning glistening with salt and health to cry, 'Hey, when's lunch/tea/supper?'

'How about a motel next time?' she suggested after a third vacation in a rundown timber shack with sagging stretchers, broken flyscreens, and a kitchen with not quite enough crockery.

'Are you nuts?' Fred had replied, still jovial from a session at the beach pub where he had run into a mate from Red Plains. 'Couldn't possibly afford it. Not with this mob. How's the roast going? I could eat a horse!'

'Well, that's good to hear,' Lannie said. 'That's what I'm serving.'

He missed it.

She settled in at work. She was efficient. People thanked her. She enjoyed a day spent in the company of adults, even those as spurious as radio personalities. She could take that with a laugh! They raised her wages.

Three months, four, five, six.

Johnnie had left school after a disastrous final examination and was apprenticed to a garage mechanic. The second eldest now had his driving licence and was actively encouraged by Fred to take the rest of them over to the coast every clear weekend. It gave him a break. Changes had gradually taken place. The boys helped minimally round the house to avoid their father's snapped impatience. They ate a lot of takeaway food. Fred grew to love those emptied weekends and spent more time in Red Plains where he took solace from one of the young women working in accounts. She appeared undemanding and pliant and believed Fred to be wrongfully used. How *could* she? she would ask his injured receptive eyes. *How could she do that to you?*

And how could *he*?

If he thought about it, and he didn't think about it too much, he might have wondered if gossip-embroidered stories of his newly acquired comfort had filtered through to his wife and kids. There were occasional nudges at pub bars, hearty male tacit wink/approval, oblique innuendoes from councillors at coffee breaks.

'How's the wife's job going, eh?' Briceland would ask with bogus concern. 'Coping, is she? Are *you*?'

Once when he had taken Norma (he called her Cuddles) home for a weekend away from the observant bright eyes of Red Plains – and anyway, it was cheaper than driving miles to some out-of-the-way motel – he had been surprised by the early return of his kids from the coast.

'Who's she?' Chappie demanded, watching Cuddles cope with a week's washing up. He was nearly thirteen now and worried by hormones and acne.

'A workmate. We're catching up on council business.'

'Er er!' Chappie said, unbelieving.

Fred installed a dishwasher.

In September Cuddles announced to Fred that she was pregnant. Even though Fred was blind to these matters – his couplings with Lannie had been more in the nature of quick relief, what he jokingly called among his buddies 'the marital piss' – other council staff had been eyeing Cuddles' thickening waistline with interest. 'Putting on a bit of weight, love.' And, 'You'll have to go on a diet, Norma.' Kidding her in the staff canteen. She repeated her news again over a dreadful meal in a Red Plains steakhouse. He didn't seem to have heard the first time.

'Well!' he said unsatisfactorily. 'Well!' He clicked a finger at the waitress for the bill and bustled Cuddles out halfway through the mince.

He had her dismissed that afternoon with a small lump of severance pay to sweeten the departure. He didn't see her again. When she went up tearfully to his office he was unavoidably away on shire business. Cuddles drove her misery out to Tannum Sands where her elderly parents, both crippled by arthritis, had retired to a nursing home.

'I wish we could help, dear,' her mother said. 'But as you can see we can hardly help ourselves. You really should have had more sense.'

Cuddles found sanctuary in a church refuge.

Seven months. Eight.

Almost every weekend now Fred went out to the coast, driven by guilt and the necessity to obliterate thinking; but Lannie, eager to avoid a surfeit of his presence, organised overtime at the radio station and left Fred sitting bleakly in her rented house, somehow sad, somehow comic in his efforts at renewing a lost cause. Once he took her and the boys to dinner, but at another low-rent steak-house that so vividly recalled his last meeting with Norma – he thought of her as that now – he could hardly eat a thing.

'You don't seem well, Fred,' Lannie suggested as she poked dead vegetables about.

'I'm okay.'

'You don't seem okay.'

'Lannie, come back home. Give up this stupid job. Your place is with me and the boys.'

The boys were all practically men, she told him, beyond cuddles – he winced at the word – and being tucked in.

'No,' she said. 'I'm being paid for working for the first time in twenty years.'

'Marriage isn't about being paid.'

'No. It isn't.'

Rumours had reached her through the boys and the occasional refugee from Red Plains she ran into in Rock-hampton. She refused to speak of these rumours to Fred. She kept tabs, but indifferently.

Fred would drive back to Drylands each weekend poised on the edge of an emotional cliff. Norma was gone yet after-yarns lingered.

Two months later Johnnie Cunneen rose early to begin his bike ride in to work at the Red Plains garage. As he went out the front door, the house slumbering behind him, he saw a neat bassinet on the verandah and in it, tucked warmly under rugs, a sleeping baby. In a carrier bag alongside was a supply of feeding bottles and napkins.

The baby whimpered once or twice and went back to sleep. There was a note pinned to its bunny rug. *Dear Fred*, the note said, *this is yours*. It was signed *Norma*.

'Hey Dad!' Johnnie cried, sprinting inside. 'Hey Dad! There's something here for you!'

Fred stumbled from his bed through the intricacies of bedding and bad dreams to find the nightmare complete on the verandah. A hundred metres away he could see his eldest son opening the first of the paddock gates.

'Oh God!' he cried aloud. 'God!'

He crumpled Norma's note, picked up the bassinet and carrier bag and took them out to his car. He could not fight the impulse to look into the bassinet, and found the crumpled rose-leaf face of the baby shuttered in sleep. His child. His. 'Oh God,' he whispered again.

Then he went back into the house and ruffled the dreams of his kids by yelling that they'd have to get their own breakfasts. Something urgent had come up at work. He'd be back as soon as he could to get them to school.

Before the first sleepy acknowledgement he was gone and in his car, savaging the miles between him and the Red Plains hospital, mentally running through a series of plausible lies, of explanations while he drove. He wondered about the sex of the baby but rammed the wonderings back. He had always wanted a daughter, a biddable property, a hostage to old age. He groaned aloud as he drove.

A nurse at reception seemed bewildered when he handed the bassinet across.

'I saw this car pull out from the shoulder,' he tried to explain. Words seemed incomplete. 'As I was driving in and when I reached the spot . . . well . . . here this was.'

The nurse was looking at him in a disbelieving way, as if she were trying to construe the situation. She asked if he had managed to get the car's number. No, he told her. It was all so sudden. The baby howled between them. 'Was there no message?' the nurse persisted. 'Nothing?'

Another, older, woman had come along the corridor and joined them and was making clucking noises over the bassinet. Fred felt his mind breaking apart. He thought longingly of the gloom and the comfort of the confessional.

'Nothing,' Fred said. 'There was nothing. Look, I really have to get going. I'm sorry I can't give you any more information.' His hands were shaking and he kept them in his pockets. He listened to his heart speed up.

He was going to add further words, platitudes like 'You'll handle this?' or 'I can leave this safely with you?' but thought better of it, nodded in a business-like manner and turned away to his car.

'Just one moment, Mr Cunneen,' called the nurse, who knew him at least by sight. But he ignored her and drove off, hands unsteady on the wheel.

In his office later that morning he found himself unable to concentrate on anything. He was ill from strong coffee. The hospital had rung asking for more details. He couldn't bear the curious timbre in his secretary's voice as she switched him through. He had been glossily abrupt. The police sergeant rang, trying a man-to-man approach, and had his head snapped off.

He went to a small café in the Red Plains mall for lunch and found himself throwing up after the first bite at a sandwich. 'Oh Jesus,' he almost prayed as he mopped messily at tabletop and clothes. Torn every which way he tried to calm himself with a righteous condemnation of Norma. How could she abandon . . .? Leave me holding the . . . ? A mother's duty . . . Who else? She must be suffering post-natal . . . He couldn't cope with the granite of facts. The child was his. His. He tried blinking moral responsibility away. It was hers. Hers. It was always the woman's.

He went to the post office and found a pay phone and dialled Lannie's work number.

'Look, Fred,' she said. 'I'm really busy now. Can't it wait?'

'There's something I've got to tell you.' He yearned for confession and absolution. He was being eaten up.

'Tell me later,' Lannie said. 'I really must go.'

The line was bad and he could only catch every second word. He thought it was his wife speaking but she

235

had already hung up and he realised it was himself stammering and dribbling his guilt into a dead line. He kept clinging to the phone like a drowner, leaning giddily against the wall of the phone box.

Meanwhile Norma was blindly driving her own desperation away, sustained by the aggrievement of the misused and the rancour of revenge. She had no money, no job, no friends. Out to the coast she drove, unthinkingly, down past Gladstone, Gin Gin, Childers. Past Bauple, Gunalda, Gympie. Not noticing the scenery, the cars, caravans, tour buses, hauler trucks, unaware even of the weather, to lose herself in Brisbane.

And then?

MEANWHILE . . .

Yes, stories were formed with words, spoken or written – even pictures, she argued inwardly, presuppose words. The oral tale-teller had an extra form of punctuation: mime, the smile, the raised hand, the frown, the tantalising pause.

But she noticed new trends on the flat page. The simple sentence (forget the old compound and complex) was slathered everywhere with its subject/verb/object, until the sensuous seeking mind reeled back from the *dum dum dum* of the rhythm – if it were that! – and the trendy immediacy of present tense. A reader recovered after doses of Austen, Dickens, Trollope, even (Lawd a mercy!) Scott, followed by a brandy chaser of Nabokov or Cheever.

She'd been reading Marshall McLuhan and his theories on the printed word leading to the separation of the

senses, and how radio and television, in fact all the elec-
tronic interplay of image and sound, would return man's
sensory reactions to the pre-print era of tactile and auditory response. It was difficult to tell whether he was for
or against this development. Development or regression?
Which? Reply! Reply! Or was he merely a sardonic
observer of doom? That. It had to be that.

She reread the accusation that print led to 'the separation of the senses, of function, of operations, of states
emotional and political . . .' Hold it, Marshall baby! You
know you're wrong.

Out there, yes, out there all over the wide brown land,
was a new generation of kids with telly niblets shoved
into their mental gobs from the moment they could sit up
in a playpen and gawk at a screen, starved of those tactile
experiences with paper, the smell of printer's ink, the
magic discovery that black symbols on white spelled out
pleasures of other distances.

It . . . was . . . frightening.

Even now, ten minutes before closing time, the per-
cussive clangour from the pub's television rocked her
flat, made the air shudder with a fogged disturbance that
seemed to have the walls in a bear-hug and be shaking
them from side to side. A sour trumpet serenading a
commercial rose above the endless repetitive bass thump,
like a cry from her own throat.

It was hopeless trying to squeeze ideas out during

that racket. She made herself more tea and jammed the window tight against noise that still seeped in like conscience.

There was a sameness about country folk and a different sameness about those in the city. She thought about that, about the group-herding that led to a kind of social monotony, those claptrap patterns in which everyone believed, articles of faith abnegating the right to individual difference: city folk were fast movers and talkers, their eyes beady for the main chance, their palms itching for quick profit. It was the done thing to denigrate them as go-getters, insensitive to others. Similar stereotyped myths attached out back: country people were supposed to be slow-moving, open-hearted, slow-thinking, maybe, but hey, salt of the earth! And looking the same, those old bushies, under their akubras, eyes narrowed from squinting against sun and peering uselessly for rain. Laconic. Using disaster for punch-lines. Given to the tall yarn – an oblique humour. Country folk were all, all the same people.

Townies. Bushies. For a long time they'd been like different races but now, as the world shrank, they were being driven uneasily together by the dominating culture of the screen.

Perhaps that talk about the global village was doomfully right.

The racket from the pub stopped. Janet opened the

verandah window. There were voices out in the street now, the banging of car and truck doors and the hacking coughs of old engines revving up. She watched the lights go out downstairs and another sad single light come on in one of the upstairs rooms. Clem was coping without Joss. But was he liking it here any better than she was? The grind of the expected. The din pulverised each day.

If only those drinkers would pick up a damn book and savour the stretch of simile, the rock-shock of metaphor.

'The hell with the tactile and auditory!' she said aloud, listening to a pub late-leaver break wind and begin retching in the street below. What about an intellectual response, Marshall, huh? What about a stretch of the imagination? Those old brain cells forming their own pictures?

Janet went back to her bedroom and tucked herself in with her small radio plugged to her ears, twiddling the dial until she found the faintest echo of an FM wavelength working its way through a programme of Borodin. The main street and raucousness of the Lizard's patrons became part of an uneasy slumber that was ruptured by the sound of a body tripping and falling on her back stairs.

She got up and opened the landing door cautiously, squinting blindly into the dark well that led to the yard behind the newsagency. Then she flashed her torch on steps, walls, and the moving shadow created by the ground-floor door swinging uneasily on its hinges. She flicked on the outside light to the yard and went down into the hot night and found the lock had been damaged, the doorknob itself hanging limp like a broken fist. The yard yawned empty.

She went through to the shop. The books she never sold were mute on their racks, the pawed-over magazines lay in the piles she had neatened before closing time, the unsold papers were bundled ready to go back on the morning truck to Red Plains. Nothing had been disturbed. Cards, toys, stationery – untouched. She went over to the cash register. Its bland face ignored her. She opened drawers. Petty cash lay unwanted.

Is it me they're after?

Why?

Did they suspect she was slandering the town?

There had been those continuing offhand questions over the last couple of months: What you do up there all the time, love? Must get you down. Hear you tapping away. Writing a book, eh?

Friends, she would reply. Writing to friends. Rellies. The tax. And grin amiably.

But she wasn't writing a book about them. She was

writing about what could be about them. The possibilities of them. Fiction, she guessed, amplified the 'what ifs?' of everything. She could look out her window at the main street and think, What if this should happen, or that? She was making the players act beyond the boundaries of what she knew and what could be, moving them centre stage or back into the wings, urging them to preposterous solos in empty halls, the audience gone, the orchestra packed up, discarded tickets chattering in the small dust-winds along the footpath. She was the constant among variables.

She went to the back door and slipped the bolt she had forgotten before going to bed. The lock could be fixed – today, she realised, looking at her three o'clock watch. But that wasn't enough, she told herself with an admonishing 'Was it?' Time to go, she decided, boiling up water for a quick fix of caffeine. After all this time.

A five-year bite. Five years of not quite making it. Add on those years spent with Ted on the farm not quite making it. It was time to go.

But where? That was the problem. She could sell at a loss, lose the few friends she had made during that decade and vanish to some undisturbed hamlet by the sea. If there were any left.

The town was changing. Groups of teenagers hung around till nearly midnight skateboarding along the brief strip of bitumen. Last month a brick had been put through her window and that of the sad haberdashery store run by Lily Barnes. Two elderly pensioners had been mugged in their own homes. The nearest police station at Red Plains took its time sending someone out to investigate complaints. What a town! she thought. And once I loved it. The council had moved Benny Shoforth on and, every now and again, Sergeant Dorgan came out and harried the fringers from farther west who camped down by the creek when their own fishing-holes vanished in the dry. The fringers moved and returned with the persistence of yoyos until Dorgan threatened them with a quick run to the lock-up.

Farmers were selling up, distraught by lack of water, dying stock and impossible debts. One couple had been forcibly removed by the bailiff, the bank hovering ogre-faced behind the whole procedure while kids howled and the mother wept and the cheap furniture on time-payment was dumped outside. They had got into their beat-up car and rattled away along the gravel roads until their petrol ran out. Where were they now? Janet couldn't bear to think, remembering the cruel television coverage that stripped them naked.

Suddenly she found herself aching for the sea.

ALMOST THERE, ALMOST HOME

'What do you really think of Alban Berg?' the woman in the ladies' lounge asks as she sips her brandy and dry.

Listen, sweetie, I want to say but don't, I've had it up to here with cricket scores, lousy wickets, groin injuries, suss referees' decisions, and I don't give a shit about anything except wishing the sporting blah would stop stop stop. I'm not unreasonable – remember this is a female point of view – but I do think this country is round the bend over jumping and kicking and running and swimming and smashing into people all in the name of winning. It isn't about sport any more. It's about power. And money. And politics. And it's boring. My God, it's boring.

And there's those bimbo shows that come with it, the antipasto, the cheer squads looking as if they're on leave from some strip joint in the seedier part of the Valley. I mean, well, they don't seem to be able to run any games at all without a dash of sex and a lashing of grog. All those hunks in the change-room after matches squirting each other with champers, a kind of dick substitute. God! How it must excite the barflies envious of a 750ml bladder.

Christ!

I stop wiping over the plastic surface of the next table and look at her. 'Who?'

'Never mind, dear. The composer.'

'Oh, him.'

I'm at snapping point, what with the bloody cricket going on and on and on in the main bar and the men reaching the nasty-drunk stage and Clem refusing to lower the sound.

'They like it. They don't want to miss an over. Only another hour to go, Joss. Be a love and bear with it.'

Suddenly I find myself sagging down at a table and staring at Paddy Locke enjoying her solitary glass, and I give her a smile so fragile it has a further dampening effect on the whole gloomy room with its green wall-paint, deep brown varnish trim and pictures of forgotten show bullocks.

Above the cane planter and its plastic ferns is a blown-up sepia photograph of the Rock, taken circa 1910, before the town was fully formed. (You can see the silverfish lunching behind glass.) There was an economic boom for a while. Now the town's returning to its foetal stage and Clem refuses to see it.

There are no other customers in the ladies' lounge. The few women who drink at the Lizard stay in the outer bar with husbands or boyfriends. I can't blame Paddy Locke for requiring me to walk those extra metres to serve her. She's sheltering from sports fallout.

'It's im-bloody-possible in there,' I say. The old tmesis. I wonder if Paddy Locke knows the term. I bet she does, if she knows the name of some composer no one has ever heard of.

Paddy Locke is another dimension in this town. A kind of failed intellectual. She's tried for years to interest the ladies – I have to use that word – in culture. (Forget the blokes.) Music groups, drama groups, reading groups. Brief flutters of interest till every venture died its natural death. Why bother? Why try?

That's what I'm afraid of – apathy. I tell Clem I must get out before it takes over and I'm in there with the rest, glued to a screen, tossing back liquor anodynes and roaring with the punters as some bullneck from the Broncos makes it for a try.

Why am I here?

I did all the usual things for a Brisbane city girl: private school (Mother: 'You meet a nicer type of person.' I didn't), and then the old humanities degree that was ultimately useless as far as putting a meal on the table. At least I could *read* those unemployment charts.

In a bold sideways move I enrolled in a hospitality course and learned the elements of conning visitors to our shores, followed by an additional semester in a Tafe cooking class. Exhausted by all this but armed, I felt, as well, I did the next orthodox thing and went overseas to backpack my way through the kitchens of Europe. A mistake. It was hard to get a job, even of the most menial kind, and before the money ran out I decided to come back via the States and bus my way from New York to the West Coast.

Clem, my husband, Clem of the Legless Lizard, is a Yank. Actually, that's a misnomer for a Deep South gentleman like Clem whose daddy owned a café just off Bourbon Street in New Orleans.

Fatigue made me decide to stop for a while in that schmoozy town. I found a cheap room in a back street, kept counting the last of my travellers cheques, and wandered about watching the pavement artists in front of the cathedral trying to con all the visitors from Nebraska and Michigan who were down south hunting for dat ole watermelon banjo-pluckin darkie stuff and finding they were watching blue rinsers and retirement paunches from Iowa and Montana who'd come south for dat ole watermelon banjo-pluckin . . .

Every day I went round to Vermillion's to eat because the food was good. I went for the cheapest dishes. I ate chicken gumbo till it came out my ears and breakfasted each day on corn on the cob. After four days they got to know me. I felt they were waiting for me to turn up. They had a lot of regulars. 'You're late, folks,' Clem would chide an elderly couple who always arrived about the same time as I did. 'Why don't y'all find some other place, huh?' And the husband would grin and snap back, 'We caint! We promised ourselves we'd eat bad,' and Clem would laugh and give them the best table in the room and speed back to the kitchen.

Clem was helping his daddy – I have to say daddy, they all do – run the place. Clem was a Vietnam vet, a tall handsome fellow with what I can only describe as the mellowest of manners.

'Brisbane,' he said when I outlined my origins. 'Hey, I know Brisbane. Spent my last leave there. It's a great little town!'

That's one nice thing about Americans. They're so polite they'll lie about almost anything. They don't want to hurt your feelings. So we swapped stories, became friendly, and the next time I went in Clem tore up my check and said, 'On the house.'

'I have to go,' I told him after three weeks. 'I'm missing home. And I'm broke.'

'Listen,' he said, 'why don't we get married?'

That gave me pause. Clem was aeons older. Mid-forties. He'd done it once and his wife had vanished with a boatie working the Florida Keys. He was what one might call a happily divorced man.

'I want to go home.'

'Let's both go home, huh? Daddy's pulling out of here at the end of the year. He's nearly seventy-five and I guess you could say he's had it.'

'But doesn't he want you to keep the place going?'

'I think he's kinda lost heart since Mumma died. You know how it is.'

We stared at each other for one of those long buzzing silences.

'Listen,' Clem said again. 'We get on fine. I'd like to see that wide brown land of yours, down under, like you folks say. If it doesn't work out, why, honey, we'll have a great parting, two cars with ribbons going in opposite directions as fast as they damn well can from each other, with cards on the back saying "Just Divorced" and a zillion people cheering and throwing confetti. How about it?'

He made me laugh. That's what I liked, like, about Clem. He can always make me laugh.

Well!

I rang Mother in her Gold Coast hideout.

'I'm getting married,' I said.

'You're crazy,' she said, and hung up. She'd had a bad time with Father.

Elderly Mr Vermillion was sweetness itself, grey drooping moustaches like a replay of William Faulkner. He threw a wild wedding party for us that included every regular who'd been going to the café for years. There were a few petty crims as well, a couple of girls working from a house off Canal Street and who, I guess, had comforted Clem with freebies over the years. Who was I to object?

The café was sold within a month and Clem and I set off to Saint Augustine to help move his daddy in with his younger widowed sister who lived in one of those pretty white clapboard houses near the sea. I liked it there too. I could have stayed. But Clem was adamant in his madness to get away, as obsessed as I had been to get there.

Travelling is a delusion.

'We can buy a little hotel. Make it into really something.'

I kept my counsel. He didn't know about our back-country pubs. Now in the aridity of dust and dying sheep I comfort myself with small sea-winds coming off the Gulf Coast and colder winds from the Atlantic and tree-lined streets in that old Spanish settlement, drowsy in spring with magnolia and live oaks and green lawns and timber decorations on the dormers and the turret icing-sugar of the houses. Two places mixed up in my heart, New Orleans and Saint Augustine.

Clem was as drunk with newness in my country as I had been in his. Outback, he kept saying. I want to see the outback.

Properties were cheaper there than in the glitz of Brisbane or any of the coastal towns. We drove west and west and north and south of western points to settle finally on this rundown six-bedroom wreck in Drylands.

'No lease, honey.' Clem was jubilant. 'I can buy the thing outright and do it up. Could need to borrow for that.'

We met locals. We dealt with councillors and a slippery lawyer from Red Plains. The laconic quality of language and business dealings drew only cries of pleasure from Clem.

'I can't believe this stuff!' he would say. 'Too much!'

There followed weeks of scraping, painting, scouring. Later Clem had a satellite dish erected on the pub roof to trap every nuance of every game played in the whole goddam country. We employed casual help for the bar until Clem found a newcomer, Franzi Massig, who had a small acreage out of town. He was willing to act as yardman, bar-help and general dogsbody.

No one used the guest-rooms except a teacher at the local primary school who stayed for a month because he couldn't find cheap enough accommodation in Red Plains, and a few reps travelling through when the Red Plains motel was full.

'This isn't a paying proposition,' I suggested to Clem after eight months.

'The bar is.' Clem ran slender fingers through his hair. 'You Aussies are certainly great drinkers.'

I wouldn't argue that one. But the town! It wasn't really a town. It was more a hesitation in the road. There was a post office with a petrol pump outside that Mrs Friske manned in between sorting mail and handling dole cheques. There was a tiny café, a haberdashery store that sold next to nothing but was there, I guess, for the look of it and to give Lily Barnes an identity. Every now and again I'd pop in to buy a scarf or hanky or maybe a card of buttons, not because I needed them but to offer Lily a sense of purpose along with a yap about the weather.

Across the road from the pub was a newsagency and another fifty metres east was a hardware store with a convenience section of groceries and vegetables run by Mrs Councillor Briceland. Everything appeared to be running at a loss. Weekly a line of semi-utes, vans, beat-up trucks and dodgy cars exploded dust on the road to Red Plains to stock the larder. Only the properties south of here seemed to use our townlet with regularity, as if the extra thirty kilometres into Red Plains was too much after bumping in along unsurfaced tracks.

'Counter dinners?' Clem suggested in a moment of madness. His fingers did a little blues riff on the table. 'Friday night buffet?'

The dining-room was just off the ladies' lounge and separated from the kitchen by swinging doors. Love those swinging doors! Clem had updated the kitchen but mainly for our own convenience and it was hardly equipped for commercial cooking.

We tried dinners and failed all within a fortnight and the table covers were put away again, leaving only one corner set up for Clem and me who ate, it must be said, in a catch as catch can fashion.

'Anyway,' – I was looking for excuses – 'we'd be taking custom from the caff. Can't tread on commercial toes in a town this size.'

But did we tread on each other's?

The spotted mirror in the upstairs bathroom we have not yet got round to refurbishing gives me back my morning face. A five-years-on face. My usually eager features are acquiring a look of dissatisfaction. I have begun blonding my hair. It doesn't help! Clem's optimism and strange exuberance in exile – I call it that – are beginning to wear me down. These days I feel I live in the basement of his interest.

There's a routine to the running of the Lizard. Clem and I both work the bar, Franzi cleans and helps out. I manage a counter lunch of sorts – after trying a few exotics like tapas and antipasto (total failure: 'Hey, what's this wog food, love?'), we've settled for sausage and mash, chops and mash, curry and mash. They go down a treat.

Each day has its predictable contours.

I have a once-a-year week with Mother at the Gold Coast. 'I told you so,' she says.

I try making friends in the town. This is hard work. Paddy Locke looks at my desperation in an amused and friendly way. 'I'll think of something,' she says and runs me off to a concert at the coast, a discussion group on the politics of persuasion (I ask you!), a pottery class, a painting class, a film discussion group with clips.

Maybe I'll think of something.

And I have stopped working the bar at night.

I have stopped because of the drunken overtures of two local hoons who made their move on me before they realised Clem was my husband. He blacked Ray Friske's eye and bent Clutch Dallow's nose when he observed them, one sottish evening, testing my resisting neckline. They still come to the Lizard but there's a lingering resentment of both of us. 'We was drunk, mate,' Clutch said in a half-apology a week later. 'Didn't know she was your missus.'

There's a twenty-three-year gap between Clem's age and mine, though I decide, as I gaze at my evening face, it narrows, it narrows.

Five years of this town. Will there ever be a break? I ask myself, I ask Clem. Hang in there, honey-chile, he says abstractedly over breakfast, over snatched late coffee in our room before lights out. He does a Deep South drawl with elongated vowels. Hang in.

Why?

'Just a couple more years and we'll break even and get the hell out, huh? Maybe take in some place up north along the Whitsundays. It's crawling with tourists.'

'But you actually like it here,' I insist, I nag. 'Admit it! You like the damn place. And you hate tourists.'

There's a masochistic streak to Clem that defies explanation.

Clem waggles his gentlemanly skull, unwilling to confess that the whole idea of the flat western landscape has become his skin, his carapace, and that the people who move through his day are totally necessary to his own landscape with figures.

My landscape with figures is penitential.

Paddy Locke has talked me into watercolours as a soother. Clem smiles benignly. I insist on a mid-week day off to catch those shifting purples and blues of landscape that change even as you watch.

So each Wednesday morning for the last month I've been driving out miles towards the Rock, my painting gear and a large flagon of water on the passenger seat with a packet of sandwiches. There's an easel in the boot. I sing as I drive. These sun-struck days are a benediction.

This last morning: the sun is at full tide, washing in swathes of hot bitter lemon air above the hill-lines and swinging the greys to deceptive, transparent varieties of lavender. The gidgee scrub has its own independence and blankets the foothills in an almost woolly grey. I sing as I drive and am still singing when I park the car in my usual spot, set up the easel, haul out my paints and camp stool and get to work. I'm no good at it and I don't care. I try. But there is an – is alembic the word? – alembic quality about mixing colour and washing it over the surface of my paper, in seeing some crude shadow of what I'm attempting to capture float out eventually.

The Rock has a minatory quality, juts its threat sky-wards, probing, investigating, and ignores me as I claw about its base, sing, mix paint and fail to get the essence. I ignore its threat, work for an hour or so, then nibble a sandwich and lean back against the side of the car, looking at my crude art and feeling good. And it's then that a four-wheel drive roars into the clearing, does a dust-sprawling wheelie and brakes a few metres away. Ray Friske and Clutch Dallow look out their respective windows and grin. They get out, slam the car doors and saunter over in their obscenely tight jeans.

They don't say anything. They stand, legs apart, and watch me. A small fear, like a warning wind, ripples in my chest. I put the half-eaten sandwich back in the bag and start to get up.

'Don't get up, Joss,' Ray Friske says. 'Not for us, love. We're nothin. We just come to see how you're gettin on. She's a bit lonely out here.'

Clutch grins. His wide mouth spreads open over almost perfect teeth. He's only twenty-five or so but already has the beginnings of a drinker's paunch.

'Wotcher come all this way out for?' Ray asks. 'Tryin to get away from us, eh? Bit choosey, eh? You think she's choosey, Clutch?'

Clutch nods. 'She don't say much.'

'Nah.' Ray rubs a slow finger up and down the side of his nose. 'Guess she don't like us. Her old man don't like us. You like us, Joss?'

I can't speak. The words that come are chewed up in my throat. The two of them move closer.

'C'mon!' Ray urges. 'You tell us. Don't you like us?'

I force myself up, legs trembling, watery, limp, and

make towards the paints, the easel. I'm going to shove everything in the car and leave. But an arm shoots out and Clutch has me by the wrist.

'What's the hurry, love? Not good enough for you? Not even for a bit of a yarn?'

'Yair!' Ray winks and nods. 'You ain't answered us. I don't like people who don't answer a civil question. Don't you like us?'

Clutch begins shaking my arm and I wrench it away.

'She's a stuck-up bit, all right! Thinks she's something else. Why,' he says, looking down, 'I think she's a bit scared. You scared of us, Joss, way out here, no husband around? Kinda asking for it, aren't you?'

They look at me. They grin. Ray shoves his hands in his pockets and saunters over to the easel.

'Now look at this.' He puts out a finger and smears the paint. 'Don't think you got it right, Joss. Don't think you really got the talent. Well, not this sorta talent.' He turns to look back at me and his grin isn't a grin. It's a flesh stretch without mirth, it's a slit in a cavern. 'Think we'd better improve it some.' I watch while he unzips his fly and drags out his dick and pisses on the painting. He turns around when he's finished, waggles his penis before tucking it away and smiles with the fake pride of some gallery director. 'Looks better already!' Clutch can hardly stand for his belching cackles.

Forget the easel, the paints, the camp stool.

I dart into the car, fast, slippery, lock the door and switch on the motor, revving savagely before swinging round to belt off, bumping and bouncing, along the track to the main road. Clutch gives me the finger. In the rear-vision mirror I see them, still stupid with guffaws, saunter back to their four-wheel and start after me.

It's thirty kilometres to town and only a few home-steads between here and Drylands. I drive in dry panic, the car skidding on loose gravel and kicking up such quantities of bulldust I'm hoping it wrecks their vision, chokes their venom.

At the turn-off they're behind me, horn blasting, heads stuck out the windows, choking on horse-laughs. They nudge my car with their bull-bar as I change down for the turn, once, twice, before I can get ahead out on the main road. Whooping and yowling they overtake and I can hear the screech of their tapedeck as their van blasts past, swings in front and deliberately slows.

My hands shake on the wheel. I'm sick. I want to vomit. I jerk the steering hard right in an attempt to get past and hear the hideous grind and scrape of car bodies before I manage to pull out past them. Nightmare. Nightmare in broad daylight. I drive almost blindly with their four-wheel chasing, overtaking then slowing, forcing me again and again to dodge the menacing rump of their van. They could stop me in moments if they wanted, but it's greater fun for them this way – bastards! scrots! – the constant harassing and skimming inches apart, their car-toon faces twisted with their own brand of hilarity and triumph as they howl at me through the windows while I struggle to keep control of my car on the loose surface.

Eleven kilometres. Thirteen.

They won't let up. Their spite has no end.

I'm nearing the outer fringes of Drylands and soon there'll be the sight of houses set back on their runs. I wonder if I should swing into one of those long driveways and risk someone being at home. Too late! Already I've swept past the open white stock gates of Briceland's, past the entrance to the abandoned farm of old Jim Randler, and then those brief grabs of haven are gone. For the last few minutes Clutch and Ray have let me pull ahead. A spurious safety gap. I watch in the mirror as their van accelerates and comes rushing towards me, not to pass but to press me in and in towards the shoulder and the gutter of a dried-out creek. Their horn is blasting non-stop. Closer now, and they slam the side of the car, swing out, slam again. The impact knocks my hands from the wheel. I sense the car skid on gravel, grab, screech and lose it. Their van slams into me once more and vanishes down the road in dust as my car pauses on the bank edge like a dancer, trembles, pirouettes, then topples sideways.

'This is it!' I sobbed on Clem's shoulder that night. 'This is absolutely it!'

Win Briceland driving into Red Plains for a hair appointment had seen the wrecked car, stopped for a quick inspection, and a kilometre or so further on had overtaken me as I limped my bruises towards town. 'God!' she had cried, observing my blood-smeared face. 'What on earth?'

'I don't want to talk about it,' I told her. 'Please. Just get me back to the Lizard.'

I went in the back way and up the yard stairs, ran a bath and soaked for an hour.

Clem came tapping on the door and poked his head round. His smoky eyes were full of concern. He had aged in that time.

'Go away,' I said. 'I don't want to talk.'

He hesitated.

'I mean it.' I turned the taps on full.

Clem backed away in gusts of steam and closed the door. I imagine he handled the bar on his own that afternoon. At night Franzi took over and Clem left the handling to him.

Clem sat on the edge of the bed, patted my hand then hugged me. He had heard the whole story. He talked about police, prosecution, taking over retribution himself, a sole vigilante.

'No,' I said. 'It would only make it worse. Those

bastards won't let it rest. They're bullies and bullying's their kick. I think I should go away for a while. I don't want to stay in a town where I have to keep looking over my shoulder.'

'Where then?'

'There's Mother. But really there's no room for me in that microscopic flat. Look, Clem, I'll head to the coast and hunt for a job and maybe find some place more suitable than this.' My gesturing hands took in not only the pub but the whole of Drylands, its four shops, post office, school and eighty houses. 'This.' The repeated word hissed from my lips and Clem looked doubtful because of his strange attachment.

'Another year, honey. If you could stick it out another year. We'll sell up and go south, north, wherever. Find something different. A small motel, café. That's all I know, Joss.'

Clem does the books each night. Sometimes he brings them up to our room and gives me a rundown on profit and loss and I'm reminded of a couple I saw last month in the Red Plains coffee shop. They were at the next table and he spent all coffee-time verbally working through the parts of his car with concentration on the function of the battery. He produced a pamphlet and read that to her. Endlessly. His girlfriend smoked and examined space with the look of someone dead. I have never seen such boredom. He was boring me. In the end, jealous of

267

her ability to close off and my inability to do anything except be hammered by differentials and torque and gear failures, to say nothing of that refrain about the battery like a litanic *ora pro nobis*, I got up and took my coffee to the far end of the room and hid behind a potted plant. I was sniggering with nerves.

Did she leave him? Will I leave Clem?

Truce time.

We reach an understanding.

I love Clem. I think he loves me in between pauses.

Six more months, he has said. Then he'll put the Lizard up for sale. Hey! Violins in the wings! Forget it, Clem, I tell him. There'll be other places just as . . . as . . . what's the word? Meaningful? Who knows? We might, I suggest slyly, even try a run back to Saint Augustine to catch our breath.

I'm gone within the week.

I find work behind the reception desk of another hotel. I wave certificates of suitability before my employers and announce firmly that I will not work in the bar. I can do amusing things in the kitchen, I can clean, make beds, do anything on a computer. But I will not work in a bar. Okay, the manager says soothingly, we won't ask for that. I can tell by the tinsel smile on his face he's planning a housekeeper-useful who'll be able to be flung into any staff emergency. For a cut off my salary they arrange a room at the back of the building. It's an old place, heritage stuff, favoured by regulars. Its two storeys are laced with verandahs and have a view of the river.

Clem sits outside my nine-by-ten sleeping nook and holds my hand. He's trembling and suddenly I want to cry.

'Oh Clem,' I plead. 'Hurry up and sell the damn place. Or lease it. Or something.'

'Will do, honey,' he says, suddenly chipper. Is he glad I'm gone? 'Will do. I'll be out to see you when I can. And you know, you just hop in that old car of yours when it's patched up – I'll get Franzi to run it over – and come back any time.'

Even on the verandah upstairs we can hear the roar of the television from the front bar. Clem nods towards the untranslatable whump.

'Nothing's much changed, has it?'

'This is temporary. This is desperation stuff.'

'Ah well, baby.' He grins. 'Look around. Let me know.'

He's right, of course. Nothing much has changed. I'm gone from here, too, within the month and working at a plant nursery on the Emu Park road.

I like the work. I learn to graft, to marcotte. The mosquitoes are killers. I'm living in a dying beach shack with sea-sound nosing at the louvres. Because the place is only just standing, the rent is low. At night I sweat under a sheet and miss the comfort of Clem's body. I'm lonely lonely lonely.

Although there are six others employed at the nursery the days are too crammed with work for meaningful – huh! – friendships to develop. Once or twice I catch the bus into Rockhampton and treat myself to the local amateur dramatic society's offerings. I ponder joining as a backstage runabout. I think of it and think of it and chuck the notion aside with my failed aspirations as backlands artist, and late one Sunday as I oil my aching limbs from a week of lugging compost and topsoil, Franzi Massig turns up with my car.

I don't know about Franzi. All sorts of stories were circulating in Drylands over the last couple of months before I left. He's a phoney. He's on the run. He's wanted for a scam down south. I don't believe these yarns. I do believe them.

We stand outside the sagging picket fence held up by westringia bushes and stare at the sea.

'How are you making out?' he asks.

Okay, I tell him.

The car looks even more battered than I feel.

'It drives okay,' Franzi says, interpreting my glance. His blond hair is thinning. He keeps rubbing one side of his nose with a twitchy finger.

'Come on in,' I say. 'I'll make you a cuppa.'

I look at the car once more, peer in at its split uphol-stery, its grimy dashboard, the stuffed ashtray. There's a bag on the back seat. I don't mention the bag.

I'm lonely, I think I've mentioned. Achingly bone-lonely. It's really something to have someone sitting across from me in this daggy kitchen, swapping gossip, good- and bad-mouthing Drylands.

Later we go to bed.

'It's just sex,' Franzi says, halfway through, as it were.

'It's loneliness,' I say.

Afterwards we walk outside and watch the sea grow black.

'How are you getting back?' I ask.

'I'm not going back. I've left. I'm going to vanish somewhere else.'

'Vanish?'

He doesn't answer.

'Take the car. I hate the damn thing, anyway, ever since. I've been managing with bus and bicycle. There'll be another car one of these days even more beat-up.'

Franzi turns to look at me. I can't pick out the blue of those disillusioned eyes.

'Go on!' I urge. 'It reminds me too much of what

happened. Anyway, it's a giveaway. If those two bastards ever come to the coast it's like an announcement of my whereabouts. I've got this feeling they're not finished with me.'

'Nothing's ever finished. Didn't you know?'

'No.'

'Well, take it from me. Nothing. It goes on and on.'

He walks over to the car and pats its roof in a kindly way.

'What have you done with your van?' I ask, tentatively. I don't want to seem inquisitorial, don't want to sound as if I'm back-tracking on my offer.

'Left it. Left everything. Have you noticed, Joss, how the whole little town is emptying, pouring itself out like water into sand. Soon . . .'

He doesn't finish his sentence but opens the door of the car and slides in behind the wheel.

'Thanks.' He looks up as I stand there, dark against the dark sea. 'I'll remember this.'

There's no way to express the crushing of emptiness. Emptiness puts its arms about you and gives a Judas embrace and when you move to return the pressure, to lay your head against warmth, there's nothing there. You fall sideways.

For a month or two, I was so busy and so exhausted from working at the nursery, I would drop asleep instantly to the steady sea-snore and wake with limbs protesting against further abuse. I worked like an automaton, quick, accurate, unslacking. My boss, an elderly elf with a remarkable fluffiness of hair, noted approvingly. I received a salary rise. I bought a second-hand car.

'Where's the old one?' Clem asked on one of his monthly duty visits.

'I gave it away.'

'Oh yes?'

'It was too much of a reminder.'

Clem nodded. He was a wise man. He probed no deeper.

Clem visits when he can. Usually he starts driving at five on Sunday morning and reaches here about nine to fall red-eyed and exhausted on my bed and sleep till noon. Recovery takes us out for walks along the beach, tea and pikelets in a rundown caff and wolfings of talk.

Drylands is dying in its bootstraps, he tells me, merely underscoring what Franzi said. Paddy Locke has put her house up for sale and is thinking of going north. The schoolhouse was burnt down the week before and the kids are being bussed into Red Plains. There's talk that it won't be rebuilt. But we are circling the centre of my fear, my discontent, simply sifting words.

'What are they doing?'

'They?' As if Clem doesn't know. I look at him and am conscious of an ache and an absence. His sandy hair is streaked with grey. The lines running from the wings of his nose towards his jawline have deepened. The insistent bone of his body makes a voiceless cry for my concern and there's a hesitancy about him that was never there before.

'Those two.'

Clem's mouth tightens into a line like twine. 'I've banned them from the pub. I won't serve them. If they want a drink they have to go into Red Plains.'

Ray works out of town a good thirty kilometres on a sheep run owned by the local member. There's lots of clout in that, lots of protection. He fences, handles the feed truck in the dry, checks the pumps at the clogging dams and is a general handyman. His boss likes him, thinks he's a fine upstanding young man. Any day now, he could be standing for preselection, I suggest sourly. Clem laughs.

Clutch, he assures me, is still working late shifts at the railway station. (That cretinous cackle!) 'I don't think,' Clem decides, 'that he's the full quid, as you guys say.'

'They're dangerous.'

'I guess so. I guess so. But what to do, huh? What the hell to do? Okay, Joss, I'll tell you. Since they've been barred, the pub's been broken into twice. The front windows have been smashed. The upstairs rooms trashed – what there is to trash – while I've been downstairs working. I've talked to the real estate man in Red Plains but he reckons the market is so slow I'll have to give the place away. Pay someone to take it, he advises with his fat real estate agent's laugh.'

'Then give it! Pay them!'

Clem pats my hand in a there-there manner. 'We'll see.'

Hatred is an energiser. It must be what sends Clutch and Ray sniffing me out.

A week after Clem's latest visit Mr McPhee, the kindly elf, tells me someone has rung and asked if there is a Joss working at the place. My complacency is ruptured.

'Who?'

'He didn't give a name.'

'Did you tell him?'

'Well, yes, of course,' Mr McPhee says, stroking a croton. 'But he hung up at that point.' He shifts his attention from the croton and fusses round the base of a fatsia. 'Is something the matter?' He moves on to a bank of Brazilian pepper trees and makes tutting sounds. 'Aphids. I think we need a little white oil.'

Yes, I tell him. Something is the matter. I give a sketch. The sketch reminds me of my last artistic endeavours and I stop mid-sentence.

'Go on, dear,' he prods gently. He's discovered sooty mould as well.

I go on. He's shocked in his elfish way.

That afternoon, as I am about to head out the gates, I see Clutch's four-wheel parked across the road. I run back through the nursery nudging pots aside, tripping on bags of fertiliser, on hose lines, and up to the McPhees' house which adjoins the nursery. While Mrs McPhee wrestles with a batch of biscuits, I pant out my fears.

'Give me your car keys, dear,' says motherly Mrs McPhee who is a clone of her husband. 'I'll bring your car round and park it here. I take it you don't want them to know which car is yours. It's like a thriller, isn't it, love?' She continues calmly dusting biscuits with icing-sugar.

I know I should say it's too much bother. I know I shouldn't involve such kindly old people, but I hand her the keys and a few minutes later she has parked my car in a shed behind the house, calmed me with tea and shown me how to drive off via a side gate on the property.

That night I cower in a darkened house in the clamour of silence. My antennae tell me something is wrong. My skin crawls. The houses on either side are weekenders rarely used. Their unlighted windows stare blankly at the sea, as do mine. I'm afraid to sleep, and shuffle round

276

in the dark wondering if I should risk going out to the car and driving off. I've parked its giveaway presence one street back where a laneway leads down between the houses to the ocean-front.

Barricaded. I know they know. I know. Any of the other workers could have told them where I live.

The flimsy door-bolts back and front don't reassure.

I have no phone. The poverty trap!

I'm afraid to leave, afraid to stay. I even smile in the dark, as my body freezes with indecision.

But what I'm waiting for comes. Ten o'clock. Eleven. Rat scratchings at the front stir me from half-doze to catch an erratic arc of torch-flash switched suddenly off, and, louder than the sea, louder than its high-tide wallowings, the breathing of bodies on the other side of the hollow wood.

'Joss!' comes behind the whisper. 'Hey, Joss! Open up. We know you're there!'

I step back, softly, softly, moving towards the narrow hallway and the kitchen. One foot at a time through the purple air. I knock a pan from the kitchen table and the clangour anchors me, pins me in the kitchen as wacky laughter breaks out beyond my walls, and there's a cousin crash of glass when the first rock shatters the louvres. Sea air rushes down the hallway. My feet seem stuck on linoleum. I can hear a hand reached round fumbling for the front door-bolt. Move!

I wrench the back door open but instead of heading up the lane haul myself over the fence of the house to the rear and crash through its side garden, snapping neglected poinsettia as I run.

I'm pursued by yoicks and shouts. One glance behind tells me they've lit up the place like a beach fair, maybe to make sure it's empty, maybe to aid their trashing. They don't seem to know I've gone. Sometimes drunkenness is a saver. 'Hey bitch!' I hear Ray shout as I reach the lanehead and my car. His voice punctures the empty seafront street. 'Where are you, eh? C'mon, you bitch! We know you're around!'

Clutch's cackle pursues over unmowed grass.

This is a replay: the film darkened, the surface scratched. Night instead of day but the sound system repeating the original horror.

My car won't start. I'm living all the clichés of Mrs McPhee's thriller. I've locked the doors and the damn engine won't fire and while I wrestle with the ignition key there comes the galumphing pound of hoon hooves that have discovered the laneway, followed by two drunken faces pressed close to the glass of the car windows as they begin to rock the thing, screeching with laughter.

I sit in my tumbril, pitched from side to side, still wrestling with the starter, riding out a terror scenario which is destroyed suddenly by verandah lights across the road and a man's voice shouting, wanting to know what the hell's going on.

As the engine fires I spin the wheel and jerk away from those dark drunken shapes, swinging the car round to slow down long enough by the shouter and hear him yell, 'I've rung the police!'

Motel recovery.

Next morning a kindly copper accompanied me back to a wrecked house; they'd urinated on clothes, floor and in the sink. There was a puddle of vomit on the kitchen table.

'I'm out of here,' I told Mr McPhee.

'You poor child,' he said, 'they won't be back. They're being charged with malicious damage and will be held pending trial. It's all right. It's going to be all right. You can stay with us if you like. Or I'll organise something else, closer to the nursery.'

I wavered. I gave in. There was a small cottage two blocks down, also staring seawards. I confronted my own dull inability to forge decisions, waiting for Clem to make a move.

He arrived the next day after a whimper phone call.

The Lizard was up for sale and he showed me a snapshot with a real estate sign hanging from a corner post on the upstairs verandah. It was one of the saddest things I'd seen.

'But who'll notice it? Who'll come by?'

'Some mug like us,' Clem suggested with a bitter smile. 'Briceland's interested. He's thinking of turning it into a heritage museum.'

'Well, let him.'

'I'll lose too much.'

'Then lose it.'

Clem gave a great sigh that appeared to empty him out. He was tired. His thin face was even thinner. He had to drive back that night for he'd been unable to find anyone to take Franzi's place. The locals were beginning to do the run into Red Plains to get drunk there. Not even the sports channel held them. And anyway there was a bigger screen in the Red Plains tavern and a bank of poker machines.

I watched him worry, all the while remembering that small town on the Atlantic coast with its white clapboard houses and a little café called The Chimes where we had sat and giggled and held hands and wolfed fish tasting of salt, smelling of the sea. Almost there. Almost home. Why did I remember now? Why? And I began to cry.

'Don't, honey,' Clem said. 'Please don't.' He seemed blocked by something he had to say. 'Look, I have to go back. Back to the States, that is.'

He watched my eyes widen.

'*We* have to go.' He gave me a reassuring squeeze.

I could feel the strength and the fragility of his ribs behind his cotton shirt. Suddenly I wanted to play them like a harp. Play my own mournful tune of loneliness. It was his father, he was telling me. He had been ailing for some time and didn't want to worry us. I nuzzled my head into Clem's chest and after a moment he lifted my face up with one finger firmly wedged beneath my chin.

'Look at me,' he said. 'We have to be off by next weekend. I've organised everything.'

'We?'

'Of course we,' he said. And then he added that we might stay for a while if that was what I wanted.

What I wanted! Words bubbled up in my mouth, foundered and almost choked me.

Clem eased me back in my chair and leant forward until our faces were almost touching. He raised his right hand and began to trace the bone of my forehead with the tip of his thumb, moving it across and down until it settled on my cheekbone where he paused and rubbed back and forth, back and forth, gently, gently; then slowly, as if he were charting some newly discovered continent, he ran his thumb on down my cheek to describe my jawbone and follow its blubbering outline even more softly, round, round, up to the point where he had started. As his thumb shifted delicately and deliber-ately to that place where he had tapped in all his own loneliness and unhappiness – I could see that now – and wild optimism, he watched me, his eyes steady.

My own eyes were as steady as I watched back.

Again his hand began its tour.

'It's not sex,' Clem said, halfway through, as it were.

'It's amity,' I said.

It was more. It was tenderness. It was love.

This was better than sex, I decided then, which had, in the reality, little of affection, little of tenderness. It was an emptying. This was the filler.

This was the edge of something.

A beginning. A middle. An end.

MEANWHILE . . .

The world, she decided, is divided into travellers and stayers. She might have said readers and non-readers, and wondered if there were some congruence between the classifications. She was bluffed by repetitiveness, by the day to day to day.

Janet leant her doldrums over the rail of her upstairs balcony and watched the empty early morning street. The town was vanishing before her eyes. Across the road, just up from the charred remains of the primary school, the Legless Lizard still dangled a FOR SALE sign like a dead flag. The doors were closed, the rooms hollow reminders of casual overnight stays. A soiled mattress, dumped on the verandah, still huddled against the railing. Some weeks back a team of workmen had appeared and clumped through the empty rooms making an assessment of the building's suitability for some kind of heritage museum. She could see the building crumbling to dust under the pressure of council waffle and postponed decisions. Bureaucracy couldn't make up its mind whether to bulldoze the school building or not. Why save the Lizard?

Did it matter?

There was a certain (she did not know how to pin down the word for it – disaffection? mistrust?) in the fewer and fewer customers who came in for their morning paper, their lottery tickets. 'Morning, Janet.' Minus smiles. Or the skeletal 'Morning!' No name. Nothing.

Three of the properties west of the town had been reclaimed by the banks. More humiliated dispossessed, their sad belongings crammed into old pickups along with baffled, yowling kids, hadn't bothered to say goodbye or settle bills. She didn't mind the latter. It was the goodbye she missed. The café down the road had closed for lack of custom.

What was wrong? What was happening?

There had been muggings in Red Plains. Two men were arrested for peddling cocaine and the head boy of the high school was discovered selling pot to junior pupils in the lavatory block. Put this down, she instructed herself. Put this all down. But her hands mind heart had lost the impulse.

Strangely she missed the racket from the bar. Had to admit that. Hated to. Evenings now had a lack of emphasis, a nothing to resent, except when the skate-board riders screeched up and down the bitumen. Earlier that week some kid had nailed a basketball hoop to the front door of the pub and the thud-thud of a ball whacking meaninglessly against the wall had driven her crazy. Two nights ago she had dragged on her dressing-gown and gone down to confront the noise-makers, careless of her appearance, sustained by rage. She stood chilled and trembling in the midnight street.

The kids had laughed in her face then danced about her chucking the ball from one to the other, making lightning passes that giddied and befuddled, and had driven her back across the road to the safety of her shop. Not one of them spoke, answered her protests; just silently, viciously played arrow-fast around her, herding her away like dogs a sheep.

She locked herself in from what she knew to be an approaching terror.

The town, as a town, was being out-manoeuvred by weather. As simple as that. Drought. Dying stock. A hard sky across which clouds massed, hovered, then rolled away to the coast. The small spatterings of rain that dropped were as offensive as spit.

She made breakfast then went downstairs to put a notice on the front door: *Closed until eleven.* She locked up and looked grimly at the racks that had once held books and were now given over to videos. She had to live somehow! Their covers, their titles, all assaulted. 'You might as well, Janet,' Howie Briceland had advised unctuously. 'It's the way to go. You won't get the kids ploughing through books when they can get a quick buzz by flicking a switch.'

That decided her. That and the increasingly leached quality of living.

At nine she had an appointment with a lawyer in Red Plains to see about transferring the newsagency franchise to Howie Briceland's wife who had expressed interest, as they say. 'As they say!' she said aloud with a downturn of the mouth. 'As they say!' – confirmed by a phone call the previous evening. The words that had festered for two long months determined this inevitable end.

Where had all the goodwill gone?

We're leaving, Ted, she said to her long-gone husband as she bucketed along the gravel to Red Plains. We're getting out.

This sudden abandonment of sentimental loyalties to the place made her weepy.

Perhaps I should remember this moment, this landscape, should try to hold this endless line of red dirt and grey scrub as something to recall, to return to after I've left it. Once, when she was ten, twelve, she had been driving with her mother through a green valley in northern New South Wales, a valley so beautiful with its sunny iris caught between the azure lids of hills that she had consciously, oh so consciously, stared hard and deeply at it, telling herself she would stamp it in her mind for later recollection. She summoned that moment now while the strengthening sun struck the Rock full on its weathered face and momentarily revealed a figure, a something, watching the morning world. A phantom of light and shadow that was gone in moments. She pulled over by the fence-line and watched the vision fade under a blast of shifting luminosity and the ripping cries of crows.

Her business didn't take long. After she had signed papers of transfer and banked Howie Briceland's minuscule cheque she walked down the main street of Red Plains and went into the Western Rose for a coffee. Briceland had given her a week's grace for removal but while she sipped and looked unseeingly through the smeared glass of the café she knew the time would be less than that. It wasn't dust she wanted to shake off her feet but memories.

She had no idea where she might go. Only that she must.

There were a few friends in the town but she now felt

so alienated from the life-pulse, if it were that, of the last decade that she intended to leave (Hey! Cut the fanfare! The bunting! The balloons! The round of farewell drinks and insincere – well, maybe not all – goodbye speeches from unsure hosts!) quietly, not like those shamed bank-busted settlers with their tatty bedding, worn mats and drunken fridges exposed for all to see on the trays of their trucks. Two days ago Paddy Locke had thrown a farewell lunch. Only three turned up: Lily Barnes, Win Briceland and herself. 'Not like old times,' Win had complained. 'Not a scrap. When we all came with a plate, a gift. Dozens of us. Remember?' The world, Janet remembered, had appeared to be a glut of chicken mornay and cream-filled sponge. Everyone united by robust goodwill. At the end – her sort of end – there was so little that could be taken. All she would be ferrying across the frail borders of time would be boxes of books, records and pages of typing worked over as anodyne, the residue of lonely evenings.

'Morning, lady!' a loud voice hooted with jocular irony. And she looked up into the face of Win Briceland who planted her assured behind in the seat opposite, lively with new enterprise.

'Well, this *is* a day!' Win kept dabbing at ladylike perspiration. 'Something for me to get my teeth into. I must say I'm a bit tired of hardware and veg. Howie says he'll put Toff in to handle the store – it's his last year and the stupid kid doesn't want to go on to uni – so that'll free me for handling the agency. I'm really looking forward.'

She smiled complacently. 'And what about you, Janet?'

'Time. Just time. I haven't any ideas really.'

'Something will turn up.' Win could think of nothing but her own prospects. She gave Janet a sly look. 'Weren't you writing away? Putting it all down? You'll have lots of time for that now. New places. New ideas.'

Janet bent her head over her cup.

'You know,' Win said, 'I went to a couple of those writing classes. Some young woman came through. Remember? But I thought it was a waste of . . . well . . . life, I suppose. I mean, people these days don't want to sweat over something for days, do they? Like reading and such. What they want is something quick. You know. Turn it on and watch and get the story straight away.'

Janet looked up at the open simple face opposite.

'You've got a point,' she conceded. It had taken her more than fifty years to get any ragged sort of a story at all.

'Yes,' Win went on, 'this young woman, she talked about the death of the novel. Maybe she had something. Afraid I'll just be going for the newspapers and videos. Can't lose that way, eh?' She couldn't stand the silence of the woman facing her. 'You know, there's a lot of hypocrisy about. All those greenies blaming us for land clearing, felling the trees and so on for grazing. What about paper? What about that? A lot of trees for paper.' She smiled and reached across and patted Janet's hand. 'We'll miss you, love. Part of the place now.'

No, Janet thought. Not. I'm still the outsider.

'I have to be getting back,' she said. She rose and went over to the cash register and paid her bill, gave a small handwave to Win Briceland and went out into the shadowless street.

She drove quickly along the goodbye road.

Mulga. Bloodwood. Gidgee. The stayers. The ones that kept cropping up after fire, after felling. Would she, would all the others who had been drifting out and on, crop up so well? When she came into Drylands' main street the empty pub seemed to have stopped breathing. Its FOR SALE sign dangled lower and flapped uneasily in air-shift as the day's temperature rose.

She drove round to the rear of the newsagency, parking in her usual place in the back lane. The yard door shifted slightly as if to greet her and a small quiver of unease crept round her stomach. The back door swung ajar and she could see the screwdriver marks in the wood of the jamb, the splintering around the lock. She pushed the door wide. 'Hello!' she cried. 'Hello!'

Nothing.

She forced herself to go in, slowly now, cautiously along the little passageway to the shop. She could feel the emptiness. The nothing space. Every shelf of videos had been emptied, the racks of magazines gutted, the small supplies of writing materials and greeting cards removed. She had cleared the cash register before she left but the few dollars in loose change that had been in a drawer beneath were gone.

She was delighted to find she didn't care, not about any of it, and sat down on the stool she kept behind the counter for the quiet times – and there had been little but quiet times – to survey a kind of victory, a kind of defeat.

Shabbiness defeated her. The shop. The town. The empty street outside in the brightening late morning. And in addition the meaningless quality of her years. The victory would be in leaving.

After a while she rose and went upstairs, listening for movement, hardly caring if there were. The whole place had been trashed: drawers turned out, kitchen cupboards, bookshelves. She stepped across mounds of down-flung paperbacks over which had been emptied the contents of tea and flour canisters. Her typewriter sat grimly on her work table, and beside it a loose smothering of pages of writing she had been working on during the last six months. Everything was shuffled out of sequence, and she grinned sourly as the term 'deconstruction' blazed instantly and briefly. The ultimate *roman trouvé*! A killer deal for the academic.

On the top page of this pile, a final evaluation, someone had scrawled in texta 'GET A LIFE!'

She picked up the discarded pen and sat, legs wobbly, hands jittering, hoping for the ultimate reply.

She would never find it.

There was a house she had seen once in a tiny forgotten settlement on the edge of a coastal lagoon somewhere north of Brisbane. Its two storeys listed towards the sea. Its cock-eyed roof was as insolent as a navvy's cap. There was a name on a board beside the front door – Bateau Ivre – and the house, the name, the memory of the lonely sand-shore with its dripping she-oaks had stayed with her over the years. Rimbaud! Miles from anywhere! Refinding would be like the search for the ultimate Eden. For Elysium, Asgard, Heaven. Quests, crusades, illusory ideologies crumbled and ran away like sand.

She looked around her own drunken room and her hand, drunk on the pen, hesitated to write beneath the scribbled admonition the words 'TOO LATE'.

Suddenly she began laughing. She couldn't stop. It was the pointlessness of it all. And more savagely, the point made by the unknown adviser. There was something out there, but she doubted she would ever discover. The idiocy of her wasted years made her laugh even more.

There were no endings no endings no